CHAPTER 1

Elle

I'd like to think my past doesn't follow me around like a shadow on a sunny day that I just can't outrun. I have a good life. I'm smart, have a great job, long legs, perky boobs, and I've been told the guy I sort of date is a catch-and-a-half on more than one occasion. So why is it that as I look across the room, scanning for William in the crowded restaurant, part of me hopes he stands me up? What twenty-five-year-old wants to be stood up? One that will continue to coast through life on autopilot, unless circumstances in my perfect life force a change. Perfect is highly overrated. I'm a character in my story, going through the chapters of my life as if it was written by an imaginary person, when I should be the author.

I've been this way for a long time. I make responsible choices. My life is neat and organized and my heart rate stays constant. I like it that way most of the time. I should be proud of where I am in my life. But the truth of the matter is sometimes I feel like I'm suffocating in my perfunctory life.

William catches my eye and raises his hand to me at a table in the far corner of the restaurant. The one we almost always sit at. Same time, same place, every week, week after mundane week. I notice the two girls sitting at the bar near me, eyeing William and giggling. Their faces drop when they realize he's waving at me and hasn't even noticed them. I put on my best fake smile as William, always the gentleman, stands as I reach the table. He kisses me on the cheek and wraps his arm around my waist with a familiar touch.

"Sorry, I'm a little late." I say with rehearsed speech as I take my seat.

"No problem, I just got here myself." William replies, and I know it's a lie. William Harper would never be late. I'm sure he was here fifteen minutes early and since I'm twenty minutes late, he's probably been waiting more than half an hour, but he would never complain.

"Can I get you a drink?" The attentive waitress smiles at William, even though her speech is directed at me. If I were the possessive type, her overt flirting would probably piss me off. But I'm not. Possessiveness and jealousy would be emotional reactions, something I've spent years working to restrain.

"I'll have a vodka cranberry. Diet cranberry, please." I look to William and notice his glass is already empty. I inwardly smirk, thinking how well I know this man. He nurses the single drink he allots himself, a vodka tonic, for a solid half hour, then he switches to water.

"Just water for me, thank you." William smiles at the waitress and she beams from his attention. William Harper is a handsome man. You'd have to be blind not to see that. Tall, blue eyes, blonde perfectly coifed hair, and always dressed like he just walked out of GQ magazine. His teeth are white and perfectly straight and dazzle from beneath his perfect smile. He comes from a respectable family and at only twenty-seven he's already a partner at his dad's law firm. So why is it that right now as he speaks, I'm seeing his lips move, but I can't hear a word he's saying?

"Elle, are you okay?" William senses my distance and I know the concern in his voice is genuine. He truly is a great guy, a catch-and-a-half as they say.

"Oh, I'm sorry." I pretend I just snapped out of a daze. "My head must still be in the case I was working on." I lie.

The answer seems to satisfy him. "What kind of a case is it?"

It didn't take long for us to get on the topic of work, it never does. I should be happy we have our work in common and he's someone that understands what I do, but work is pretty much all we ever talk about.

"It's an unlawful termination of employment case." I latch onto the first case that pops into my mind. Luckily the waitress comes back and sets down our drinks and asks to take our order, giving me more time to think of something interesting from the dull case that I just told William my head was stuck in.

The waitress leaves and an older couple approach our table. "You're Bill Harper, Jr. right? Bill's son?" The gentleman extends his hand with a friendly smile.

"It's William, but yes I'm William Harper Jr." I've heard him correct dozens of people over the last few years. I've always wondered why it bothers him so much to be called Bill or Billy, that he feels the need to correct people. I mean, when someone uses a nickname it's meant to be friendly, isn't it? William has the polite manner in which he corrects people down to a science. Somehow it doesn't come off as rude. It's telling that I wonder why it bothers him, yet never ask.

The two men chat for a while and in less than ten minutes William manages to solicit the guy's legal work and the man promises to call the office the next day. The way he does it doesn't come off as sleazy ambulance chaser type speak. William is smooth and professional. It probably comes naturally to him, being his father, grandfather, and brother are all lawyers too.

We finish our dinner without interruption and our conversation is easy and natural. It's been that way since we met in our last year of law school. We clicked instantly and I would categorize him as one of my closest friends, if I wasn't sleeping with him once a week for the last eighteen months.

"I rented *Possible Cover*. I was hoping you'd want to come back to my place after dinner." It's just like William to rent the latest action movie, which he will most likely despise, because I am an action movie junkie. William is more of an artsy-Woody-Allen-type-movie person.

"Can I take a rain check?" I see William's face wilt slightly. This is the second week in a row that I'll be cutting our date off after dinner...and before sex. "I have to be in the office at 6am to prep for a deposition." I feign disappointment in my voice as yet another lie flows freely from my lips.

I'm not sure if he buys my excuse or if he's just too polite to call me on it. But I don't care. I'm not in the mood tonight. The last few months our sex life has become a challenge for me, although William doesn't seem to have any idea. It's not his fault either. He has good equipment and it operates well, for the most part. But I've been having trouble getting myself to my happy place during our nights together lately. Maybe that was part of the problem. If I wanted a happy ending with William, I had to get myself there. He just doesn't seem to be able to get me there on his own anymore. So I seem to have become one of those sex-once-a-week women who have to fake it. And I'm not in the mood to fake anything else tonight.

CHAPTER 2

Elle

My co-workers at Milstock and Rowe are an eclectic group of people. William and I did our internship here in our last year of law school. After graduation William went on to his father's Madison-Avenue-type law firm that was started by his grandfather more than seventy years ago. The firm is well established and caters to the elite advertising industry. Leonard Milstock, the namesake in Milstock and Rowe, offered me a position as a junior associate at the end of my internship and I happily accepted.

William and I don't disagree often, but we argued quite a bit when I had decided to stay at Milstock and Rowe. He didn't think it was a good career move to take a job with such a small unknown firm. But I was comfortable there and Milstock allowed me to do work that most junior associates at a big firm could only dream of getting their hands on. That was one of the perks of working for a small place, and I thought it outweighed the low salary and lack of prestige. William, on the other hand, thought the scale tipped completely in the opposite direction. Salary and prestige were high on William's career priorities. Not so much on mine.

"Morning Regina." I smile at the receptionist as I walk into the office fifteen minutes past the official start time of eight. No one seems to care that I'm perpetually late, especially since I usually stay until long after seven on most nights. Timeliness just isn't my thing.

"William called, he wants you to call him back. He had me check your calendar to see if you're available for a consultation for a new client of his."

Damn. Now he knows my early morning deposition was a lie. "Regina, would you mind having Gigi call him back and book whatever he needs on my calendar?" I raise my eyebrows at Regina and she knows what I'm asking and smiles, excited to be in on whatever it is that I am asking her to do.

Regina has been our receptionist for almost a year. She's in her late forties and has eight cats and way too many cat themed decorations at her desk. From the outside she looks like your ordinary middle-aged woman. A little on the heavy side, with pants that spread just a bit too tightly over her plump ass, a penchant for floral, flowing crepe shirts, and comfortable flat shoes. To the eyes, the package she delivers seems to fit the bill. That is, until she opens her mouth.

I've never met another woman in my life that has a sexier voice. For that matter, I don't think there's a man with a sexier voice either. The sound that comes out of her mouth is the purr of a sex kitten, not the roar of the teddy bear standing before you. I am absolutely, one hundred percent positive she could earn a million dollars a year being a phone sex operator, or the voice for audio erotica books. Men are rendered powerless to deny her when she asks for anything in her sultry voice. I dubbed the woman with the irresistible tone Gigi.

I'd solicited the assistance of Gigi's god given gift on more than one occasion. Sometimes to have her call clients when I knew they would be upset with my having to cancel an appointment last minute. Somehow when Gigi called in her sexy voice, the male clients took the news much better.

No one in the office knows how Regina and I met so many years ago. They probably all think she's a friend of my mother's because of how different we look on the outside. But she's not; she's my very best friend…the woman who saved my life. Although if you ask her, she'd tell you I saved hers. Who knows, maybe we actually saved each other.

Leonard Milstock is my seventy-five-year-old boss. I've only met Frederick Rowe, the other half of Milstock and Rowe once. Yet his name stays on the door and rumor has it he still receives a salary each year. The two men had been best friends since grade school and partnered up together before I was even born. Apparently Mr. Rowe was the Felix to Milstock's Oscar and kept things flowing smoothly in the office. But he'd retired a few years back due to his wife's ailing health and now all we had was the messy half of the odd couple.

I enter Leonard's office and attempt to find a chair under the piles of files with papers haphazardly sticking out all over. I remove three suit jackets I am positive have been there for at least two years and hang them up as Leonard begins to talk about the case we're working on together. As he talks, I reorganize all of the files which had been left ajar on the chair and throw out a dozen Wall Street Journals that have dates more than a year old. Leonard either doesn't notice my tidying or it doesn't bother him at all, because he doesn't miss a beat as he brings me up to speed while I go about tidying the place.

"You're going to have to handle the deposition yourself this afternoon." Leonard wraps up the discussion while chewing on a sausage and peppers hero that Regina delivered a few minutes ago, even though it's only ten thirty in the morning.

"I can do that." I can, but I'm surprised that he is asking me to. The afternoon deposition is for one of our largest clients and usually Leonard leads and I take a back seat. Leonard sees the question written on my face.

"I'm having angioplasty this afternoon." Leonard waves off the comment as if he had just told me the time and not that he was having serious heart surgery.

"Angioplasty? Are you okay?"

"Yes, yes. I'm fine. The doctors today make a big deal about nothing. He probably just wants me on the table because his kid's got a tuition payment due."

"So it probably doesn't have anything to do with the fact that you eat a sausage and peppers hero every day for breakfast then? It couldn't be that you haven't taken care of your heart, right?" I stand, assuming the lecturing daughter position that Leonard, on rare occasion, has allowed me to act out when his unhealthy habits rise to disturbing levels.

"Listen missy. When you get to be my age, we'll see how much you give a shit about what you eat. So keep your salad-eating, skinny thoughts to yourself and go prep for our client who I'm counting on you to please."

I laugh, knowing Leonard isn't really mad, it's just his way. Neither of us do warm and mushy, but he knows I care about him. "Tell Millie to call me when you're all patched up, okay?" Yes, Leonard Milstock married a woman named Millie, which makes her Millie Milstock. I would have kept my maiden name, but I'm sure that wasn't even a consideration when they married more than fifty years ago.

"Yeah, yeah, whatever." I smile at my boss and shake my head watching him finish off the last of his hero. When they scope out his veins I'm pretty sure they'll find whole pieces of sausage are causing the clog.

CHAPTER 3

Elle

A few days later, Regina buzzes into my office to tell me that William and Mr. Hunter are here for their eleven o'clock appointment. Of course, William is fifteen minutes early and me...I'm running late. I do my best to wrap up the case I'm working on quickly. I recognize I've been taking advantage of William lately, almost daring him to call me on my lies and lateness. But he doesn't. He won't mention that he caught me in yet another lie the other night when I said I had to work early, and I'm not sure if it's because he doesn't care or if he really is that polite.

"Thank you Regina, would you please show them to the conference room for me and tell them I'll just be a few minutes." I buzz back.

"Sure thing Elle." Gigi responds back to me in her sex kitten voice, definitely not Regina. I smile, wondering if she is letting me know that they are not happy to be kept waiting and she is going to appease them, or maybe Mr. Hunter is a nice looking older guy who calls for Gigi to make an appearance.

It's only a few minutes after the hour when I make my way into the conference room, which is early for me. I'm actually pleased with myself for being timely. William and his client both stand as I enter and I get the sudden urge to salute both men for some reason. My hands are filled with my coffee, notepads, cell phone, and laptop. I don't even look up at the men until I have arranged my pile on the conference room table.

Regina comes into the conference room and purrs, "Can I get you gentlemen some coffee?" No sign of Regina, she's still in Gigi mode.

I look up at William, half expecting to find a scowl on his face the way Gigi is pouring on her act so thick, but he's smiling at me in his usual friendly demeanor.

"Elle, this is Nicholas Hunter." William motions to the man sitting next to him.

I finally look up at the man sitting at William's side and I'm startled at what I find. The man knocks the wind right out of my lungs. He is quite possibly the most handsome man I have ever laid eyes on. William, who is sitting right next to him, is no slacker in the looks department, but this man is everything that William isn't. Tan skin, deep green eyes, unruly dark hair, and a rugged jaw frames the man who extends his hand to me.

"It's Nico, nobody calls me Nicholas except this guy," Nico motions to William with his thumb, "my mother, and my priest." He reaches over the table and extends his large hand to me. My petite one gets lost in his and it feels like I'm shaking the hand of a man with a baseball glove on. His handshake is firm and warm and he looks directly into my eyes as he speaks, a slightly cocky smile on his face. I feel the warmth spread from our joined hands through my body and parts of me tingle as the heat finds its way to my most private of areas.

Nico. The sexy name matches the sexy man. It isn't lost on me that it must kill William to call the man Nico, knowing he has such a befitting formal name available to him. But I think Nico matches the man before me much better than Nicholas. I'm staring at him, but not just because he is utterly gorgeous, I feel like I know him from somewhere. Even the name is familiar, Nico Hunter. I'm sure I know him from somewhere, but the appointment had been with Nicholas Hunter and that name didn't ring any bells.

"Elle?" William calls my attention back to him. I hope I wasn't staring for too long. And did I have my mouth hanging open too? That would just be rude.

"Nicholas, umm Nico, has an endorsement contract that he wants out of. My firm has taken a look at it, and it looks ironclad to us from a contract prospective, but we thought maybe you could apply the Weiland case to this."

Interesting. Weiland was a case that I wrote a paper on in my last year of law school that was published. It was a big deal for a student to get published outside of law review, so I'm not surprised that William remembered the case. The case was about an athlete who had a three-year endorsement contract with a company that sold an energy drink when he signed the contract, but later merged with another company. The other company manufactured a drink that was marketed as a drink to mask the use of performance enhancing drugs. Weiland didn't want to be associated with a company that touted masking performance enhancing drugs from testing. Unfortunately his contract was airtight. But in an ingenious move by his attorney, rather than sue alleging one of the contract terms was invalid, which he would have lost, they sued based upon a violation of the contract's moral clause.

So Nico is an athlete of some sort? That's not surprising by the way he looks. He's a large man and I can tell he's in great shape even with a suit covering his body. "Why don't you give me a little background, Nico?"

I can't wait to hear his story for some reason. It's more than just for a prospective case, I'm curious who the man is in front of me.

Nico starts out by telling me that he is in mixed marital arts. I don't really know what that entails, but I assume he means some sort of karate expert. As he talks I try to take some notes, but I find myself staring at him, unable to move my eyes to the paper to write. When he speaks, he looks directly into my eyes and it makes it even harder to break our gaze. I forget William is sitting right next to him. There's no one in the room but me and the man with the deep green eyes who won't give me a break from the intensity sucking the energy from my body.

Regina enters the room with coffee for our guests and I'm grateful for the break as Nico turns his attention to Regina to say thank you. When Nico turns his attention back to me, I glance up at Regina who looks back from the door then looks between me and Nico and wiggles her eyebrows suggestively. I pretend to cough to cover my smile with my hand and William offers me his water. Always the gentleman.

Nico picks up where he left off and I take a minute to get a better look at his face before he locks my gaze with his again. I notice a small, healed scar above his left eye and another longer one on his right cheek. They are faint, like they've been there for years, but his tan skin color yields a lighter shade to scars, making them stand out more than they normally would. The scars make his face look even more rugged and somehow emphasizes the masculinity of his chiseled jaw. The face belongs to a strong man, a man I can't take my eyes off of for some reason.

William speaks when Nico is done and his voice finally makes me remember that he's in the room. I hope I wasn't drooling while his client was speaking. I try to focus on William as he talks, but my eyes keep wandering back to Nico, who catches me each time. I see an ever so slight twitch at the corner of Nico's mouth each time, secretly acknowledging that I've been caught.

William is able to refocus me by drawing me into a conversation about how the Weiland case could apply. Nico wants out of an endorsement contract he is in because the manufacturer uses child labor. The fact that the man is willing to give up what amounts to a multi-million dollar contract for such a noble cause makes him even more sexy to me.

After almost an hour, William looks at his watch and begins to wrap things up. Nico asks me my opinion on his case and I tell him I need a copy of the contract and some time to do a little research on the company before I can give an educated opinion.

William nods and stands, "Are we on for Thursday, maybe we can discuss it further then?"

"Umm, yes." I catch Nico looking between the two of us. I think he is observing our interaction.

Nico shakes my hand again and my heartbeat speeds up at the simple contact. He doesn't release my hand right away. Instead he uses his other hand to motion between William and I and asks, "Are you two a couple?"

I respond no at the exact same time that William responds yes. I look to William and then to Nico, who is still holding my hand from our handshake, and I think I catch a glimmer in his eye that matches the smirk on his face. He's amused at our answer and I don't blame him. He finally releases my hand and I find myself oddly disappointed that he's not touching me anymore.

I turn to William and find he is still looking at where Nico's and my hands had been joined. His face looks conflicted and confused and I feel badly for the disrespect that I've just shown him. He lowers his voice to me, "I'll see you Thursday?"

I nod, thinking it best to have whatever conversation needs to be had between us in private. I stand at Regina's desk as the two men walk out the door. Nico looks back at the last second and smiles at me. William never looks back.

I toss and turn all night, unable to get the picture of Nico Hunter out of my head. The man is sexy as hell and it bothers me that I can't control my thoughts. It feels like I only fell asleep ten minutes ago when I wake up to the music blasting on my phone alarm. I drag my half-sleeping body into the shower and let the cool water pour over me in an attempt to force myself awake. After a few minutes of self inflicted torture, I adjust the temperature on the water and close my eyes to relax into the warmth. It hits me then. My eyes dart open, trying to force out the picture that appeared from the darkness of my memory without warning.

Nico Hunter. Nico "The Lady Killer" Hunter. I was there the night that he killed a man. It was the one and only fight I'd ever gone to. And it all comes flooding back. I referred to the fight as the cage fight, but now that I think about it, it was called MMA, mixed martial arts.

My stepfather is a retired policeman. Sometimes he works security at sporting events, a lot of retired cops do. He had been given two tickets to a big MMA championship fight, and offered them to me. I wouldn't normally go, considering my past and how I feel about watching people pummel each other, even if it is consensual. But my little brother Max is a huge fan of the sport and I got suckered into taking him. I just couldn't say no to the excited twelve-year-old who momentarily forgot he was supposed to act cool and was jumping up and down like he did when he was four.

The fight didn't last long, two rounds. I remember it clearly. It was probably less than ten minutes in total. The pre-fight festivities lasted an hour longer than the actual fight. Our seats were good, only about 10 rows back from the center of the ring. I remember flinching every time one of the men threw a punch, yet I couldn't turn away. I close my eyes and watch instant replay of those last seconds. Most people think having a photographic memory is a blessing, but in my case it's a curse. Yes, I remember lots of figures and words, but I also remember all of the bad things I'd rather forget.

It's as if I flipped on a video and hit play right as those last few seconds play out. I see Nico throw the punch, and then I watch in slow motion as his opponent's head turns to the side with the force of ten men. He drops to the floor, his head limp and rattling around before it even hits the canvas. The screaming crowd becomes silent and the medical team rushes into the cage seconds after it all happens.

As horrible as it is, seeing that all play out in my mind isn't what haunts me. It's the still of the fighter dropped to his knees when he realizes the man isn't getting back up. He's shattered. I can't take my eyes from his face as I watch him break into a million little pieces. I should've felt sorry for the man that just lost his life, but I don't even look his way. I'm fixated on the man who will never be the same. Never. I know it. I feel connected to him for a stopped moment in time.

In my mind, it's high noon and the shadow of my past is twice the size of me. Towering over me. I can't escape it.

CHAPTER 4

Elle

I'm later than usual when I finally get to the office. I'm still in a fog and find myself dazing out as I catch up on emails and plan my day. Nico "The Lady Killer" Hunter. I didn't know him before the fight, but that was his name. I remember watching him walk into the cage and smile a cocky smile at the crowd. The ladies went crazy. It didn't take long to figure out what his name meant. I remember feeling a jolt when I took in his smile and that body, that incredible body.

The press had a field day for weeks after that fight. His name may have been Nico "The Lady Killer" Hunter before the fight, but the press removed the "Lady" part from his name after that.

I'm typing words into Google before I even realize what I'm doing. The pictures that were etched into my brain are no different on the screen when they appear. The referee had ruled the fatal blow a clean hit, but that didn't stop the press from sensationalizing the story. A few weeks later, after the press had moved on to whatever carcass was yet to be picked over, I read a small story hidden in the back of the paper amongst the advertising. Nico's opponent had had an unknown underlying head condition and was a walking time bomb.

I'm able to push thoughts of Nico into the depths of my head and finally get some work done after two more cups of coffee. It's midafternoon when Regina buzzes in to tell me I have a client in the lobby, but I don't have an appointment on my calendar.

I walk into the lobby, my thick sandy blonde hair being held in place on top of my head in a lopsided bun held together by two strategically placed pencils. I stop in my tracks as I see Nico rise from the couch in the waiting room and toss a magazine back on the table.

I'm surprised by his appearance, but he seems oddly familiar after spending half of the night and most of the morning in my mind. I put on my best game face and straighten my posture. "Mr. Hunter, did I have an appointment with you today?" I pretend I'm concerned I may have forgotten an appointment, but there is no way I've forgotten anything about the man from the two times I've seen him.

He takes two steps closer to me, just an inch or two closer than one would consider normal space between people. But I notice it. He's taller than me by at least eight inches, if not more. "It's Nico, please." He smiles at me and the room feels smaller, warmer.

I smile back. I don't have to fake it, it's a real smile. I'm happy to see him and I can't hide it anyway. I have no idea why. I should be freaked out after what I remembered, but I'm not for some reason. I'm curious about this man. I nod my head. "Nico, what can I help you with?"

He smiles, it's a mischievous, lopsided smile that makes me think the man is playful. But damn if it isn't the sexiest thing I've ever laid eyes on. "I remembered a few things I thought I should tell you that I didn't mention yesterday. Do you have a few minutes?"

I tilt my head to the side and study him. What is it about him that doesn't want to make me run even though I can feel my heart racing through my shirt? "Sure, let's go talk in my office."

Nico smiles a victorious smile and it's contagious. I smile back and I'm not quite sure what we are even smiling about. He follows me down the hallway and as I turn into my office I catch his eyes lingering on my behind. He looks up just as I take in his line of sight. A normal response would be to be embarrassed at being caught, but not Nico. He grins at me unapologetically. Instead of finding it rude or harassing, for some reason I find it turns me on.

21

I sit behind my desk and Nico looks at the small chair sitting opposite my desk and back to me. "Would you mind if we sat over there?" He motions to the couch behind him and I realize for the first time that a man of his size wouldn't fit in the little delicate chair which sits in front of my desk.

"Oh, sure, I'm sorry." I let out a small laugh. "I guess that chair wouldn't be too comfortable for someone your size?"

Nico stands next to the couch and waits for me to sit. I sit on the far end and expect him to sit at the opposite end, so there is space between us as we talk. A desk usually fills the requisite space for a business meeting, but there is no desk separating us on the couch. Nico doesn't do the socially acceptable thing. Instead he sits directly next to me on the couch. Not abnormally close so we are touching, but close, like we're in a theatre next to each other.

God it's hot in this little office, I realize I shouldn't have closed the door. I stand and walk over to the window and open it. I walk back to the couch and Nico turns to face me. He's so close I have the urge to reach out and touch him. He's watching me and has a small smile on his face. I get up to grab a pad and pen and his smile is bigger when I return, he looks amused. He must realize that I'm fidgeting. I'm trying hard to pretend he doesn't affect me, but he does for some reason.

"So, Nico, what did you want to tell me about?" I put my pen to the paper, ready to take notes with my head down. I'm determined not to get caught in his gaze again.

But Nico waits quietly and doesn't speak. Eventually I have no choice but to look up at him to see why he hasn't started talking yet. And he catches my eyes when I do and smiles. I smile back, even though I'm aware he just completely played me.

"I forgot to ask you out to dinner yesterday."

"Dinner?" I'm momentarily confused.

Nico smiles a devilish smile and I get the urge to kiss it right off his face. What the hell is wrong with me? I'm calm, cool, and collected. Not some schoolgirl at a loss around the cute boy in class.

22

"Yes, dinner. You do eat, don't you?" His voice is a mix of amused and teasing.

"Umm." I stammer for a few seconds. "I can't."

His response is quick, I feel like I'm at a deposition and I'm the one being deposed. "Why not?"

"Because it wouldn't be right."

"Do you have a boyfriend?"

"Not really."

"Then why wouldn't it be right?" Nico flashes the crooked smile and I know before he speaks whatever he says will be something flirty. "I think it would be very right."

His crooked smile makes me smile and I lose my train of thought. Very unlike me.

"It's complicated." Those two little words would scare away most men, but apparently not Nico Hunter.

"Okay, let me hear it. I'll help you sort out the complication so we can get it out of the way." Nico leans back further into the couch, crossing one leg over the other, settling in for the story. Really?

"Well...you're William's client."

"And you said the other day you weren't a couple, right?"

"We're not." I'm being honest, I don't think of William as my boyfriend. Boyfriend implies relationship, more than just good friends who satisfy each other's sexual needs occasionally. But my answer isn't totally truthful either. "I mean, not really."

"Okay. He unfolds his arms and settles them on his knees as he leans forward. "So where's the complication?" He looks directly into my eyes for a minute before he continues. "In the not really?"

I blush, I'm not sure if he realizes what I'm saying or not. "Yes." I hold his gaze when I respond, determined not to back down.

Nico assesses me and takes in my embarrassment. It's emanating from me, even though I'm reaching deep for my calm, cool and collected persona. I can't seem to hide what I'm feeling from him, he won't allow it, and I have no idea why I let him control me. I can't help myself around this man and it makes me feel unraveled. "Let me take you to dinner. Just dinner. I'll be a perfect gentleman. Scout's honor." He holds up his hand and three fingers.

I furrow my brow at him. "Were you even a scout?"

"Yes." He says the word without conviction. I squint and look at his face with disbelief. He knows I can tell he is leaving out something.

"Okay, so it was only for a day. My brother and I got into a fight and got kicked out at the second meeting. But it still counts. I was a scout."

I smile at him, amused at his attestation, assessing the sincerity with which he spoke. "Why?"

"Why what?" The confusion on his face is evident.

"Why do you want to have dinner with me?"

Nico takes a slow, assessing gaze up and down my body, making no attempt to hide his blatant assault. He gives me a boyish smile that has an edge of sexual undertones to it before he speaks. "Aside from the obvious, that you're gorgeous?"

I blush, but force myself to remain quiet. A good negotiator knows when to keep quiet and let their opponent squirm to fill the silence.

"You're smart and confident and the people around you seem to love you." He stops and watches me, I can tell he is deciding to continue. "And when I look in your eyes I see a little light flicker..."

He pauses for a second. I look at him, but still don't speak.

"And for the last twenty four hours all I could think about was what it would take for me to turn that flicker into a flame."

Holy. Shit. I stare at him for a long moment. My mind is spinning, but I already knew my decision before he even spoke. I stand, silently signaling the end of our conversation. Nico stands and joins me. Waiting patiently for my response.

"Okay."

He smiles, and I'm caught in his boyish charm. "Okay?" I think I've actually surprised him.

I smile back and raise an eyebrow, daring him to question my answer.

"Friday, 7pm. Give me your address. I'll pick you up."

"I'm barely done by 7pm. Why don't you pick me up here?"

And just like that I made dinner plans with Nico "The Lady Killer" Hunter.

CHAPTER 5

Nico

"You give any more thought to taking on Kravitz?" Preach stands on the other side of the bag, struggling to hold it in place as I alternate between kicking and punching. He's been bugging the shit out of me for four months now. It's been thirteen months since I stepped out of the cage and today was the first day that I didn't wake up in a cold sweat reliving it since it happened. Nope. Instead I woke up with a hard-on and a picture of Elle smirking at me, daring me to question what had made her change her mind about going out with me. I took a cold shower. It didn't fucking help. So instead I came down to the gym and started earlier than usual.

"Are we going to have this conversation again, Preach?" I hit the bag with a series of quick strikes and catch Preach off guard, he takes a step back to steady himself. He knows damn well I meant to knock him on his ass.

"We're going to have the conversation until you get your head out of your ass and get back in the damn cage."

I switch to leg attacks. My legs are stronger and I know I have a better chance of taking him down behind the bag with the power of my legs. But fucking Preach is ready for me and his stance didn't even falter. He probably knew what I was going to do before I did. That's what happens when you stay with the same trainer for ten years. They get into your head and know you better than you know yourself. They have to. Otherwise how would they break a fighter of their bad habits.

"I'm not ready." I stop and double over with my hands on my knees to catch my breath. I've been at it for almost eight hours, but Preach doesn't know that. He gets pissed if I do anything over six in a day. Says a man's body has to rest if he wants it to renew, or some shit like that. He came in at his usual time and assumed I'd just come down.

I see a glimmer of hope in Preach's eyes when I stand to face him. I know what he thinks, I didn't say no today. He sees it as progress. I'm sure he'd take anything at this point. I know I'm a stubborn shit and haven't budged from not wanting to get back in the cage for thirteen months. But Preach knows me. I still workout six hours a day, six days a week. Fighters don't put in that kind of time unless they're training for a fight. Even then, some who are training put in less.

I didn't lie to Preach, I'm not ready yet. But today I woke up and saw a glimmer of sun breaking in from under the cloud I've carried around with me for the past year. I don't know if it will lead anywhere, but I'll be ready if it does.

CHAPTER 6

Elle

I look in the mirror at the newest outfit I've picked out and decide it will have to do. I'm already a half an hour late for work and I haven't even left my apartment yet. My bed is littered with clothes, haphazardly thrown all over the place. I must have tried on ten outfits this morning. I feel like a teenager. I never give much thought to what I wear to work or my dates with William. I have nice clothes and William and I make an easy transition from work to dinner. He removes his tie and jacket and unbuttons his top two buttons. I take off my suit jacket. But I'm not dressing for William today.

I want to look sexy tonight. I know I shouldn't care what I wear on my non-date dinner with Nico Hunter, but in the pit of my stomach I do care. I see desire in his eyes and it fuels me. I like that I can put it there, even though I don't want to. I take one last look in the mirror and like what I see. I have on a cream colored pencil skirt that hugs my body and comes a few inches above my knee. I've paired it with a soft pink, completely see-through blouse with a nude colored cami underneath. Because the cami is nude, it's not entirely clear if I have anything on underneath without a closer inspection. I topped off the outfit with nude heels. They're higher than I usually wear to the office, but because they match my skin color, there is no break from my leg to my foot, which makes my already long legs look longer.

I get the reaction I hoped for when I walk into the office, only the reaction comes from Regina and not the man I dressed for this morning.

"You look hot, Elle."

I smile at Regina. I'm a little embarrassed that I dressed for a man, but Regina is my friend and won't judge me. "Thank you, Regina." I give her a gratuitous twirl in the lobby.

"You're going to make that man wag his tail and hang his tongue out of the side of his mouth for the whole date."

Regina's words make me smile, but then I force myself to slam back down to reality. "It's not a date." My face is serious and I use my best scolding lawyer voice.

"Whatever." Regina smiles.

"It's not." I know she's pacifying me.

"I'm not arguing with you. If you say it's not a date, then it's not a date." Regina's smile never leaves her face.

"Good, because it's not." I stroll past Regina and head to my office. I have a million things to do, and now, due to my playing dress up this morning, I have an hour less to do them in.

I'm happy everyone has already left when Nico walks in the door right at seven. I'm putting files on Regina's desk as I catch a glimpse of him on the sidewalk through the glass front door. He's wearing jeans and a dress shirt and I feel my heart rate increase as he walks into the lobby. The man is sexy. Not beautiful or handsome, those words are too generic to describe what he is. Sexy. Sensual. Rough. All man.

"Hey." He smiles at me with that lopsided grin and for a second I feel my knees go weak. The man makes me feel like a teenage schoolgirl. I can't remember the last time I felt like that. Yes, I do remember, I was a teenager.

"Hi." I smile at him. I swear his smile is contagious, I just see it and my mouth mirrors his in response.

29

"I just need a minute to shut down my computer." Nico nods and I step around Regina's desk. The front reception had been hiding my body and I'm still looking at him when he catches the first glimpse of my outfit. I watch his face change and it makes my day of running around to make up the hour that I was late this morning all worth it. I head down the hall to my office and steal a glimpse back at him as I turn to enter my door. He's watched me from behind as I walked. He doesn't see the smirk on my face as I go into my office to get ready to leave.

I lock up the front door and wait for Nico to show me the way to his car. But instead he walks forward to the motorcycle parked at the curb in front of the building and hands me a helmet with a devilish smile. Really? Who picks up a date on a motorcycle?

"Umm...I can drive." I offer, thinking maybe he doesn't own a car. With gas being the price that it is and living in a city with a good public transportation system, it might even be practical to have a motorcycle instead of a car.

"Have you ever ridden before?"

"No."

"Are you afraid?" He seems genuinely concerned that I might be.

"No." I'm actually not, although I probably should be.

He smiles and there I go again, responding in kind. "Good, then get on."

I look down at my skirt and back up at Nico in contemplation. His face is amused. He slips his helmet on and casually throws his leg over the bike seating himself like he's done it a thousand times before.

He turns to me and waits, his smile still in place. I shake my head at him and put on the helmet before carefully straddling the seat behind him so as to not give anyone who might be watching a show. I'm pretty sure I heard him chuckle.

I'm not quite sure what to do with myself once I'm on the back of the bike. I feel awkward. Leaving space between us, I rest my hands on Nico's back, my palms near his shoulders. Nico takes my purse from my hands and tucks it into a saddlebag I hadn't even noticed was there.

"Scoot forward." I do.

"Wrap your arms around my waist and hold on tight." I hesitate for a second, but do as I'm told. Safety first, right?

"Put those sexy shoes on the pegs and don't move them. Not even a little."

Okay, so now I may be a little nervous. I consider asking him what could happen if I move my feet, but my thought is fleeting as he pulls away from the curb and I find myself wrapping my arms around his waist in a death grip.

After a few minutes, I start to relax. Most of the traffic has passed and it's a beautiful late summer night. The wind hits my face and it feels exhilarating. Freeing. I loosen my death grip around Nico's waist, and splay my hands around his abdomen. For the first time, I'm relaxed enough to actually feel what is beneath my hands. Solid muscle. Not just firm and in shape like William, the kind of muscles that are ripped. Swollen. Deeply defined. They're raised under his flesh and I want to move my hands around to explore better. But I don't.

We slow as we enter a neighborhood I'm not familiar with. I've never been to a restaurant in this area. William and I tend to stick to the same restaurants, exploring new ones occasionally that he finds when a new Zagat comes out each year. We crawl almost to a stop in front of what looks like a warehouse and I watch as a metal garage door opens. It looks like a delivery entrance, but Nico steers the motorcycle under the slow rising door and it begins to close behind us.

He turns the motorcycle off and takes off his helmet. I follow his lead. "Where are we?" I look around the unfamiliar surroundings as I speak. We're in a garage, there is a large, dark colored SUV parked next to us and a few bicycles hang on the walls to the side.

"My house. Well, technically we're in the gym down here, but I live in the loft upstairs."

I look at the SUV next to me as I do my best to unstraddle the bike in a ladylike manner. It's not an easy task to accomplish. "Is that your SUV?"

The sides of Nico's mouth turn upwards in a hint of his devilish grin. "Yes."

He takes my helmet, hands me my purse, and motions to the door. "Come on, I'll give you a quick tour before we go up. Dinner is in the oven, but we have a little time."

I'm still absorbing that he is cooking me dinner and we are not going to a restaurant when I feel his hand on the small of my back as he begins to lead me into the main part of the building. His large hand takes up half of my lower back and I can feel my skin underneath his hand sizzle. The hair on the back of my neck stands up of its own accord, my body buzzing from a simple touch. I don't even think he notices my reaction.

Nico flips a switch and the enormity of the room we entered comes into focus. It's the entire bottom floor of what was likely once a warehouse. But now it's a state of the art gym. There is exercise equipment in one half of the space and the other half has what looks like two large boxing rings set up.

"Wow. This is really nice. It doesn't look anything like my gym."

Nico chuckles. "I doubt any of my clientele look anything like the people at your gym either."

I look at Nico confused and he explains. "It's a fighter's gym, Elle. It's filled with men with tattoos and raging testosterone. I'd hate to see what would happen in here if you walked into this place dressed how you probably look for the gym." Nico shakes his head and chuckles.

Oh. I'm not sure if I should be offended or take his words as a compliment, so I choose the latter.

After a few more minutes, we walk into a freight elevator and Nico pulls down a metal gate. He inserts a key into the control panel and the elevator slowly ascends. Nico lifts the gate and his hand is back on my lower back, as he steers me out of the elevator and into his loft. It's enormous, almost as wide as the downstairs.

At least half of the floor is a huge open space. Off to one side is a sleek modern kitchen with stainless steel appliances. There's an oversized island and gleaming granite countertops that modernize the dark wood cabinetry beneath them. The living area takes up the other half of the floor and has the largest sectional couch that I have ever seen. I bet the couch can hold ten men. I notice it's strategically positioned in front of a large flat screen TV and I envision a bunch of guys sitting around watching fights. A complete bachelor pad, but a very nice one at that.

My nose catches a scent and I'm surprised. "Chicken Franchese?"

Nico smiles at me as he walks into the kitchen. "Very good."

"I'm impressed. You can cook?" I never gave it any thought before, but in the years that I have been seeing William, he has never once cooked for me. I'm not even sure if he even can cook.

"Don't look so surprised. I'm pretty good at it, if I may say so myself." Nico walks to the oven and checks on dinner.

"Do you cook often?" I'm so curious about this man.

"I have to, it's part of the sport. You can't keep in shape and eat crap, so you learn to cook healthy pretty fast if you're serious about fighting."

I nod, it makes sense. It's next to impossible to maintain a good diet when you live off restaurants and takeout. I should know. The only choice is salad, which is how I have been able to keep thin, but a man that looks like Nico needs an intake of way more calories than a salad could supply. "Do you still fight?" I don't even think before the words come out of my mouth. Maybe he doesn't like to talk about fighting. I remember the newspaper saying he had retired after what had happened, but he was definitely younger than whatever the normal age is for fighters to retire.

Nico tells me dinner is ready and puts out an entire meal of salad, vegetables and the main dish. I noticed that he didn't answer my question, and I'm not sure if it was intentional or just the timing.

We sit at the table for a long time after we eat. I tease him about how domestic he is and he teases me about how dependent I am on takeout. He laughs when I tell him I'm on a first name basis with at least five deliverymen. Our conversation flows naturally and time goes by fast. Too fast. Eventually we relocate to the couch and our conversation turns to how he got into MMA. Nico tells me he's the youngest of four boys and was raised by a single mother who worked two jobs.

"I got my ass kicked a lot. My mom was at work at night and my brothers were into wrestling big time."

I laugh at the notion that Nico could get his ass kicked. "You? I hate to see what your brothers look like."

Nico laughs, "I was always big for my age. When I was eight or nine my mother would warn my brothers that some day I was going to be bigger and stronger and get even with them for the years of ganging up on me. I don't think they expected that day to come when I was only twelve."

"How old were your brothers when you were twelve?"

"We're all two years apart so they were fourteen, sixteen and eighteen."

"You were bigger than the eighteen-year-old at twelve?"

"I don't know if I was bigger than him back then. But I could fight better. I remember the day that it happened too. Joe, the eighteen-year-old, came home and I was drinking out of his cup."

"His cup? He had his own cup?"

Nico laughs. "It sounds worse than it is. But yeah, he had a cup and none of us were allowed to drink out of it. I used to take it out when he wasn't home and pour a big glass of milk and dunk my cookies into it."

"On purpose?"

"Yeah, on purpose. I liked to use it when he wasn't home, it gave me a secret satisfaction." Nico smiles and shakes his head, realizing how silly it sounds to have taken satisfaction from using someone else's cup. "But one day he came home early and caught me. We went at it like we usually did. We broke the coffee table and the end table wrestling around. Mom used to get pissed when we broke the furniture. But after we rolled around for a while, I pinned his ass to the floor."

I smile watching Nico tell his story with such fondness in his voice. I'd never heard anyone speak of fighting with such reverence. To me, fighting has always meant hatred and violence and ugly things. But oddly enough, when Nico speaks of his brothers he makes it sounds like it comes from love and beauty.

Nico stands, "How about a glass of wine?"

"Sure, I'd love that."

Nico brings me a glass of wine, but nothing for himself. "Aren't you having one?"

"I don't drink when I'm training." He sits next to me on the couch, much closer than he had been before. My leg touches his inadvertently when I lean forward to set my drink down and when I look back at Nico he's looking at our legs where they meet. He notices me watching him and he brings his eyes back to mine. I'm mesmerized as he looks into my eyes and then slowly his eyes drop to my mouth for a long moment. I can tell he's forcing his gaze back to mine against his will when his beautiful green eyes refocus on mine. His eyes are dilated now and my breath hitches when I see my own desire reflected back at me.

"Oh." I swallow hard. What were we talking about? Drinking. Drinking while training. "Are you training for a fight?"

Something different passes over his face at my question, and I'm not sure what it is. "Not really." Nico ponders for a second. "But if you ask Preach, he might say differently." He chuckles. The mood has changed and I'm not sure if I'm disappointed or relieved.

I lean forward and take another sip of my wine. "Preach?"

"He's my trainer."

I wait for more, but nothing comes. "Why would Preach think you're training for a fight if you aren't?"

"Because he thinks he knows me better than I know myself."

"Does he?" Nico is surprised by my question. I watch as he thinks before he responds. I like that he doesn't just spit out an answer. He seems to consider his words carefully.

"Maybe. I've been with him since I was fifteen. He does know me pretty well."

"He started training you when you were fifteen?"

"No, not at first. When I was fifteen my mom lost her second job, so my uncle got me a job at a gym so I could help out. Preach hired me to clean up and hold the heavy bag while the fighters trained. One afternoon, the regular sparring practice guy didn't show and I talked Preach into letting me fill in. I was good at blocking shots from my three brothers, so it wasn't hard for me to catch their shots with the pads. I did that for a little while and then one of their best fighters, who I thought was an arrogant asshole, took a cheap shot at me while we were sparring and it pissed me off, so I hit him back and we went at it. I wound up kicking his ass and the rest is history. Preach started training me after that."

We spend the next few hours talking about my work and Nico's family. When he finally drives me back home, the early morning people are already out jogging. The whole night flowed effortlessly, without any uncomfortable moments until we're in front of my apartment building.

Nico parks his bike and helps me off, not releasing my hand when I'm off. He stands close and looks down at me and I think he's going to kiss me. But instead he leans down until I feel his breath on my neck. My whole body responds and I lean in against him ever so slightly, but it's enough for my body to be grazing up against his tight chest.

His mouth is so close to my ear, it sends shivers down my spine. I want him to kiss me so badly, but don't want to want him to kiss me. His words are a whisper in my ear as he speaks. "I'd love to see you again. You let me know when the not really turns into a solid no."

My body is in heat from being so close to him. I'm disappointed he doesn't kiss me, but relieved at the same time. He's right for reminding me about William. Nico releases the hand that he is still holding and I smile up at him before I turn to walk away. I take a few steps away from him and turn back. "Why did you pick me up on a motorcycle if you have an SUV in the garage?"

Nico looks down sheepishly and then I see the cocky lopsided smile that just melts me somehow. "I wanted to feel your arms wrapped around me tightly."

Right. Damn. Answer. He'd kept his word all night and been a perfect gentleman. I smile at him and begin to turn to walk away, but my feet take me back in the other direction. They seem to have a mind of their own. I need to feel him once more. I rush the four steps it takes me to get back in his space. Nico doesn't move, he stays still and watches me intently. Waiting. I reach up and press my lips firmly to his and the electricity that had been threatening my body all night zaps to full wattage. Sparks. Fusion. Jolt. It overpowers me. We instantly melt into each other. Nico wraps his arms around my waist, our bodies pressing firmly against each other, neither of us able to get close enough. His arms are locked so tight, there's no way I could escape if I wanted to. But I definitely don't want to.

When we finally break the kiss, we're both panting. Nico leans his forehead into mine and I catch my breath enough to speak. "I wanted to feel your arms wrapped around me tightly, too."

Nico smiles at my words and I turn to walk away. I really don't want to walk away, but I know if I don't, I won't be able to very soon. I walk up the stairs feeling his eyes on my ass with every step and my hips put on a show as they sway with renewed enthusiasm. I open the door and look back to find him watching me and not ashamed to let me know it. I shut the door and lean against it. What the hell am I doing?

CHAPTER 7

Nico

I'm up at five a.m. every morning. Well, every morning except today. I slept like shit, my body a mass of pent-up frustration. I kept my word all night. Even though all I wanted to do was pick her up, carry her into my bedroom, and ram myself into her to claim her as mine. Then she kissed me. I know I could have taken it further after that kiss. But I don't want one night with Elle. I want more. I have no idea why, but I do. A lot fucking more.

By the time I drove back home last night, I'd gotten myself under control. I'd reasoned with my hard-on until it finally saw my way. Who knew you could reason with a fucking hard-on. I guess I never tried. I just took care of it, did what it wanted me to.

But then I walked into my loft and I smelled her. And all reasoning went out the window. I couldn't sleep with a steel pipe in my pants, so I took a cold shower. It didn't help. Then I was wide awake with a hard-on. I tossed and turned with a picture of Elle smiling at me in my head. Taunting me for being such a sap.

The constant hum of the bell from downstairs reminds me how late I am. It's almost six. I buzz the elevator up and lift the gate and find Vinny standing there. I swear the kid grew overnight. At thirteen he's only a few inches shy of six foot already. The kid's going to be a force of nature sooner, rather than later.

"What the fuck?" The smartass kid has balls of steel to look at me and talk that way. He reminds me of me at that age, and I force myself to cover the smile. I can't let him think it's okay to show disrespect.

"Language." I say sternly.

He rolls his eyes and looks like a teenager again. "What are you, my mom?"

If I was his mom, I'd still be high from the night before. Cracked up on whatever today's loser brought with him. A different loser every day, but it's always the same story. She fucks him to get her high for eight hours. It could be bleach he hands her to shoot into her vein. The last time I saw her she was so desperate, it might have been better if someone actually gave her bleach. Put her out of her misery. The kid might be better off in the long run.

"No, I'm not your mom. But I can kick your ass with one hand behind my back, so show me some respect you little shit."

"So you can curse, but I can't?"

"I'm an adult."

"Hypocrite."

I rub my hands across my face, losing my patience after my lack of sleep. "Go downstairs and give me five miles on the treadmill. If there is any time left before school we'll train, big mouth."

Vinny groans, but quickly starts back toward the elevator. When I started training with Preach, all I wanted to do was learn moves. I hated cardio too, it was punishment to a kid who was in a room with a good trainer.

I take my time making my protein shake and make one for Vinny before I head down to the gym. I know there probably isn't any food in his house. Some of these kids only stay in school because they know they can get a free meal there.

Vinny is drenched in sweat as he runs full out on the treadmill. I smirk as I pass him. I would have done the same thing. The faster you're done with the cardio, the faster you get to the fighting.

"Preach says you might fight Kravitz." Vinny gives me a quick left and I duck and easily sweep out his legs while he attempts to rebalance from his miss.

"You're leaving yourself exposed. Lean into it. Set up your legs." I extend my hand and pull Vinny back to his feet.

"So is it true? Are you getting back in the cage?"

"Stop gossiping like a little girl and take me down." The kid needs to focus. Plus, I don't have an answer to give him.

Vinny shoots in and tries for a double leg takedown. The kid is definitely becoming more explosive.

"Nose up. Back straight. Again."

He shoots, I wobble for a second, but I don't fall. Someday kid. Someday.

After another twenty minutes, he's drenched and I'm warmed up for the day. "Jump in the showers. Make it fast. You got 25 minutes to get to school. If I find out you're late, next week will be ten miles on the treadmill and there will be no time for training, no matter how fast you run."

Vinny groans but sprints to the shower. The kid wants it bad. I just hope it's bad enough to keep him clean with all the shitstorm swirling around him at home.

"See you Monday, Nico." Vinny jogs by me with his backpack swung over one shoulder. I nod and he's gone. Out the door after a thirty second shower. I smile knowing he'll make it to school on time. I pick up the phone and call my brother to give him an update on his student. The kid's lucky my brother has a soft spot for fighters or he'd have had him expelled the last time he found Vinny pounding a kid three years older than him in the stairwell. But instead, he found him a place to channel the fighting he was doing in the halls. Yep, the kid lucked out when they assigned his teachers.

CHAPTER 8

Elle

"Sal's deli just called to see how Leonard was feeling. Business must be down with him out for almost a week." Regina says with a smile as I hand her the menu for our lunch order.

"He's probably just afraid we'll sue him for damages after they've fed him those deadly sausage and peppers heroes every day for all these years. You know how much fat and cholesterol are in those things?"

"You know who doesn't look like he eats any fat at all?" Regina wiggles her eyebrows suggestively and speaks in her best sex kitten voice.

"Nice segway. I think you can turn any conversation into something about Nico Hunter lately. You should've been a lawyer." I laugh at Regina's latest obsession.

"Do you blame me for being smitten?" Smitten, who uses the word smitten?

I sigh, thinking back to our kiss last night. No, I certainly don't blame Regina for being smitten. I think I agreed to have dinner with Nico so I could find something wrong with him and get his lethal smile out of my head. But last night only made things worse. I didn't find a single thing to help me push my wayward thoughts out of my head. In fact, I actually found things that made it harder to stop thinking about him.

"Are you going to tell me about your date or do I need to bring you into the conference room for a formal deposition?"

"How come you never ask about my dates with William, Regina?"

"Because I don't want to be bored."

"Regina!" I raise my voice chastising her.

"What?" She smiles at me knowing I'm not really mad. It's an odd friendship, but the part of my relationship with Regina that I value most is that she is so honest when we talk.

"What makes you think my dates with William are boring?"

"Aren't they?" Regina grins knowingly.

"William is a nice guy."

"I didn't say he wasn't."

It's my turn to sigh. Regina is right. My dates with William are boring. Nice, comfortable, but boring. But it's good for me. I don't need any emotional rollercoasters, I've had enough of that to last a lifetime.

I don't leave the office till after ten. I'm handling my caseload and helping out with Leonard's while he's still out. I keep myself busy all afternoon and late into the evening after my lunch with Regina. I don't want to think about Nico. He isn't what I need. I should be thinking about William. He's the type of man I should be with. He's stable, honest, and hard working. He's good for me and he cares about me. So why are thoughts of Nico keeping me awake? I toss and turn for hours until I'm finally exhausted enough to slip into dreamland.

I wake in the morning to screaming. I'm petrified. Unable to move at the harrowing sound. It takes me almost a full minute to realize that I am the one making the sound. I'm screaming and I can't stop. The dream is back. It's not really a dream, it's a nightmare. Although nightmares are a figment of a person's imagination, so I guess what I just woke up to wasn't a nightmare...it was reality. My reality. My memory. My past.

It's been six years since I woke to the torment that haunted my sleep for as many years. I can't believe it's starting again. It took me years to make them go away.

I always wake at the same place in the nightmare. His fist connects with her head and she stumbles back and hits the refrigerator. Hard. Her eyes roll into the back of her head as her body slides down in slow motion. He's really hurt her this time and it doesn't look like he's done with her yet. He leans down, his fist pulled back, ready to pummel her lifeless body. A gunshot blasts. It's so loud it hurts my head. The sound leaves a high-pitch ringing in my ears. It makes me reach up and cover them. I never knew sound could hurt. I feel like my ears are bleeding.

My hands are always covering my ears when I come to. The sound is so real that it wakes me. Every time is as real as the first time. The vision never dulls.

CHAPTER 9

Elle

I throw myself into my work to the point of exhaustion for two non-stop days. I think if I wear myself out enough, I'll be too tired to dream. Whether or not it stops the dreams from coming isn't important, what's important is they don't come for the next few nights so I don't question why.

My phone buzzes and I reach for it. I've lost track of the days.

Dinner tomorrow night? I miss you.

William always confirms our date the day before. But I'm surprised that he adds that he misses me. We don't talk about feelings. We enjoy each other's company. We talk about work. We eat at nice restaurants. We have sex. If it wasn't for the sex part, I would classify what William and I have as a great friendship. But the sex started us down a road to somewhere, although I have no idea where we're heading. I'm not even sure what William wants out of what we have. We don't talk about it. We just go through the motions and that worked for me for a long time.

I think I've hit a fork in the road and I need to make a decision. Really move forward with William or start in a new direction. I've stayed stagnant for too long.

Same time, same place? I know what his response will be before it appears on my screen.

Yes. Looking forward to it.

I've set a mental deadline for myself. I'm better under time constraints. Tomorrow night I will either break it off with William or I'll stop whatever has started with Nico. It just doesn't feel like the two can be mixed.

CHAPTER 10

Nico

Our once a month dinner at my brother's house is always chaotic. There are bodies rolling around the floor, furniture is tossed upside down and the television is blaring, but no one is watching it. Growing up my mom always said she hoped we'd have a houseful of little boys to get even with what we put her through. I look around at the seven little boys my three brothers have spawned and smile, thinking my mom got her wish.

"You want a beer?" Joe, my oldest brother, asks as he waves smoke from his face standing in front of the barbeque. We've all told him a hundred times to lower the temperature on the grill so he doesn't wind up in a smoke cloud that turns into a grill fire, but he'll never freaking listen.

"Nico doesn't drink when he trains." Preach walks up behind me and slaps my shoulder as he speaks.

Joe's eyebrows shoot up. "Why didn't you tell me you finally decided to go back in the cage. It's about time you stop feeling sorry for yourself and get back to work."

"I haven't decided to go back in the cage." I shoot Preach a nasty look and he smirks at me. He knows he's just unleashed at least an hour of lectures from my brothers and he isn't sorry a damn bit.

"Oh. You still putting in six days a week?" Joe flips the burgers as he speaks and I see the flames start to shoot higher.

"Yeah."

"Well then shit or get off the pot, bro." Joe's wife Lily walks over and yells at him to turn down the flame and he begrudgingly listens to her.

"It's not that easy, Joe, and you know it."

"Sure it is, asswipe. You open the cage door and you get in it. Then you kick the crap out of the idiot standing in the other corner of the ring."

"Oh, is that all you do? Why didn't you say so sooner?" The sarcasm dripping from my voice. I chug my water bottle and stare at my brother.

"Maybe I should kick your ass to get you warmed up." Joe almost sounds like he thinks he really could.

I grin at Lily who walks up behind Joe and hands him a plate for the burgers he's just massacred for us. She rolls her eyes at her husband's threat. "Think that ship sailed a long time ago, honey."

Joe turns to his wife. "You don't think I can take that pretty boy anymore?"

Lily pats her husband on the chest, patronizing him. "Sure you can, baby." Lily turns her attention back to me. "Nico, I have someone at work I'd like you to meet. How about you come over next weekend for a barbeque and I'll invite her?" Lily looks down at the plate as Joe finishes loading it with charbroiled burgers. "On second thought, I'll cook." She winks at me.

Normally I'm open to meeting women. I don't even ask the typical questions people want answered when they're offered a fix up. I've always been an equal opportunity man, I like them in all shapes and sizes. "Can I get back to you Lil? I sort of met someone."

Lily is surprised at my response. "You mean you're seeing someone *exclusively?*" She emphasizes the word exclusively as if the concept was foreign to me.

"Not yet."

"Well what's stopping you?"

"She is."

"Why don't you just use your usual seek and conquer charm that you always do?" Lily is only half kidding with her comment.

"Because this one you have to earn."

Lily shakes her head and mumbles something I can't hear as she walks away laughing.

"Shit, bro, you're screwed. The one's you have to earn own you."

Preach brings up the Kravitz fight at the table again and I endure another half hour of lectures and name calling from my brothers. It's the first time that I'm seriously considering getting back in the cage in a long time. But Preach pissed me off, rallying my brothers on his side, so I don't tell him. I'll let him suffer a little while longer.

CHAPTER 11

Elle

As I drive to the restaurant to meet William, I regret agreeing to dinner so soon. Two days wasn't enough time to sort out my head. I'm more confused now than I was a few days ago. I've made a mental checklist of reasons I should be with William. He's every mother's dream, tall, handsome, polite, smart, well educated, and kind. I even tried to make the same checklist of reasons I shouldn't be with William, but after hours of trying to come up with something, that side of the page is still empty. At first I thought it was Nico clouding my judgment on William, but then I realized I've been at the same place with William since long before Nico Hunter stepped foot inside my office. Maybe I just need to put more effort into whatever it is William and I have.

As usual, William is at the same table we always sit at when I walk in. He's surprised to see me on time. I smile at him, but put more effort into it than usual. Maybe this won't be so hard to do. The look on his face tells me he's happy to see me too. He tells me I look beautiful as he kisses me on the cheek and gives me a warm, be it quick, embrace. He's a good man, I know he will make a good husband and father some day.

We order our drinks and William takes my hand on top of the table. It's a bit outside of his norm. Public displays of affection aren't something he prefers, which has always been just fine with me. Softly, his thumb caresses the top of my hand. I look at where our hands are joined and watch as his thumb strokes back and forth on the top of my hand. It feels...what does it feel like? Nice. Comfortable. What it doesn't do is make my heart rate speed up. And it definitely doesn't make the little hairs on the back of my neck stand up at attention.

My phone buzzes and I excuse myself to look at it. I lie that I'm waiting to hear from Regina about a call. But I'm stalling. Waiting for a sign on what the right decision is at the last minute of my self-imposed deadline.

I can't stop thinking about you. Nico. My pulse quickens and I feel my palms start to sweat. I finally realize that all the lists I've made didn't help me decide because they've been about William and the problem isn't with William. It's me. I don't feel what I should feel about him, no matter how hard I want to.

I set my phone aside and don't respond to the text. William reaches for my hand and I pull it back. I force my eyes from the table and look up at William. He sees what I'm thinking in my face. He's a good attorney, knows how to read people, especially me. I finally stop stalling and make my decision. Even if Nico isn't the one for me, William isn't either and I'm not being fair to him.

Twenty minutes later I'm back in my car. Of course William was a perfect gentleman about it when I told him I couldn't see him anymore. I'm not sure if it just didn't upset him or if he's good at covering his emotions. Either way, I'm wearing mine on my sleeve tonight. I'm going to put myself out there emotionally for the first time in ages. I'm scared, but excited at the same time.

In my car, I take out my phone to respond to Nico, but then put it away and decide to take a leap of faith. The restaurant is only ten minutes from Nico's place. I drive with my head in a cloud, thinking about what I will say when I get there. He can't stop thinking about me. I can't stop thinking about him. Where it will take me I'm unsure, but maybe I can really give it a try. It's the first time I even want to try.

I'm happy and excited the whole drive to his place. But when I arrive, I'm suddenly nervous. I think about sitting in my car for a few minutes and regaining my composure, but I know I'm stalling and if I give myself time to overthink it I'll probably leave. I'm doing this. I walk briskly to the door and ring the bell and wait. Long minutes pass and I'm just about to turn around and chicken out when the door opens.

"Did you forget your key?" Nico is buttoning the top of his pants as he speaks and doesn't look up right away. His hair is wet and he has no shirt or shoes on. I'm silent and I don't move. My feet are stuck to the ground as I take in his naked chest for the first time.

"Elle?" Nico looks up and finds me standing there instead of whoever he was expecting.

I open my mouth to begin to speak, but a voice from behind me takes me by surprise. A woman's voice. "Hey." I turn. She's beautiful. The woman standing behind me is smiling and beautiful. My chest tightens and I feel a huge knot in my throat. Then she turns to Nico. "You going to just stand there, or are you going to be a gentleman and take the packages so I don't drop one?"

Nico takes the bags and the woman turns to me. "Sometimes you have to hit this one over the head to get him to snap out of it." She smiles and tilts her head to the side, assessing me. "I'm Lily."

Nausea overwhelms me. I didn't stop to think that Nico might have company when I decided to drop by unannounced. I smile apologetically to the woman who is still smiling at me. Oddly, she doesn't seem bothered that a woman is standing at his door as she arrives with groceries in her arms.

Feeling the wind knocked out of me, I respond as loud as I can, but it still comes out as little more than a whisper. "I'm sorry. I should have called first." I look at Nico and then to Lily and quickly turn to go. I'm embarrassed and I want to run home and throw up in privacy.

Before I can take my first step, Nico grabs my arm. "Elle, wait. Don't go." He looks confused. I want to shrink down and crawl in a hole somewhere.

"Elle?" The woman asks and I must look at her as confused as Nico is looking at me.

I look back at Nico, at his hold on my arm, and back up to his face. "Really, it's fine. I should have called. I'm sorry I interrupted." I look at Lily apologetically and then back at Nico.

Something passes over Nico's face. A look of understanding and he smiles at me. There's a glint in his eye and he looks amused. Suddenly, my embarrassment turns to pissed that he hasn't released my arm and he finds my uncomfortableness amusing.

"Elle." Nico waits until I look up at him and he has my full attention before he continues. "This is my sister-in-law Lily. She was just dropping something off." He turns to Lily to speak. "Goodbye, Lily."

"I could stay for a little while." Lily offers and I hear her smile in her words even though I don't turn to look at her.

Nico never takes his eyes off of me as he speaks to Lily. "Bye, Lily."

Lily giggles and turns to leave. She takes a few steps but then turns back to say something. "I'm going. But you better bring her to next month's dinner."

Nico shakes his head and smiles at me as he steps aside. "Come in."

We walk through the dark gym and into the elevator that leads to his loft. Nico reaches up to pull down the gate and I watch as the muscles in his back ripple as he extends his reach high. Every inch of his back is defined and two large tattoos cover each shoulder blade.

After the gate reaches the floor Nico turns and catches me checking out his back. There is heat in his eyes, it makes my breath catch the way he looks at me. He takes one step toward me and stops, but doesn't turn around to face the front of the elevator. He takes a second step, closing the distance between us almost completely. My instinct is to take a step back, to keep hold of my personal space, but I don't. I stand my ground and look up at him. My heart is beating so loudly I'm sure he can hear it.

Nico slowly bends his head and buries his head close to my neck. Arms at his side, he doesn't touch me, but he's in my space. He takes a deep inhale and I know that he's taking in my scent. There's something incredibly erotic about when he takes a deep breath in, as if he needs to absorb me into his every sense. When he speaks, his voice is guttural and low, his hot breath lands on my neck and sends a shiver down my spine, straight through to the tips of my toes. "You're here."

I look up at him. "I am." My voice is soft, but I can tell by the smirk on his face that he hears me just fine.

"Does that mean not really is a no then?" His face is serious now.

"Ask me again." I grin up at the handsome face that is towering over me, invading my personal space.

"Are you seeing anyone?"

"No." My response is assertive.

"Yes. You are."

I'm confused. "I am?"

"I don't share Elle."

"Oh." Oh my.

My pulse races as he slowly lowers his head and brushes his lips against mine ever so softly. The gentleness of his touch makes me want to pull him to me and slam my mouth into his so that I can be sure it really just happened. But I don't. I'm too mesmerized by this man and want to see what he does next.

Nico pulls his head back slightly, but doesn't step out of my personal space. "We're going to try this again." He searches my eyes before he continues. "Are you seeing anyone Elle?"

"Yes?"

Nico smirks. "You don't sound so sure of your answer, Babe."

"Will you kiss me again if I get it right?"

My response amuses him and he drops his head laughing. "A lawyer. Do you negotiate everything?"

I stop and think before answering. "I do."

Nico smiles at my truthful answer. His eyes close and he leans his forehead to mine. "God you smell so damn good."

I've never seen a body like his so close before. It just doesn't seem real. Both of his arms are covered in tattoos, it looks like he's wearing colorful sleeves, only he has no shirt on. They intertwine and wrap around his bulging biceps and I get the urge to trace a path from the first splat of ink to the last with my tongue. My body's reaction to him is unlike anything I've ever felt before. These aren't feelings that I'm used to, they seem to come out of nowhere and are uncontrollable.

One side of Nico's lip curls up slightly, as though he is amused at my staring. He hands me a glass of wine without asking if I want one and I take it because I need it to calm my nerves. I'm here staring at this bigger than life man, and suddenly I'm speechless.

The wine can't seep into my bloodstream quick enough. Half the glass is gone in one long, unladylike gulp.

"Thirsty?" I look up at him and find a glimmer of amusement in Nico's eyes, mixed with something else. I think he knows I'm trying to calm myself and I fidget in my seat on the couch as he stands there looking so unaffected.

I ignore his question and set my glass down on the table at my side. I'm trained to steer a conversation. I can regain control here, it's what I do. I push thoughts of wanting to lick his naked body out of my head and force my eyes to stay trained on his rugged face. "So tell me something about yourself, Nico Hunter. What do you like to do when you aren't training?"

He cocks one eyebrow suggestively and looks even more amused. I feel my face redden at just his simple gesture. Instead of clearing my head, he now has me thinking about what he likes to do. And I feel the need to fan myself when a visual of him doing those things to me assaults my brain.

Nico laughs and takes the few steps to close the space between us, settling next to me on the couch. He brushes a stray lock of hair from my face, pushing it gently behind my ear. There's a devilish glint in his eye because he knows what he's doing to me. He slips one large hand behind my neck, easily cupping it in his palm and his thumb remains in the front in the hollow of my neck slowly stroking small circles.

Without thinking, I lift my hands and touch his bare chest and my eyes drift closed at the hard warm feeling under my fingers. I feel the rhythm of his breathing as his chest rises and falls rapidly and I don't even realize my hands have slowly begun moving, feeling the hard corded muscle from his pectoral to just above his belly button. There isn't an ounce of fat on the man anywhere and I get the urge to dig my nails in and score him. It's totally out of character for me, the feeling comes from somewhere deep within me. A place I've cut off access to a long time ago.

Nico puts a finger under my chin and forces my gaze up to his eyes. My knees feel like jelly and my mouth is parted when I look up into his beautiful green eyes. I see a reflection of my need and I have to clench my thighs together to stop the tingle between my legs, but I can't move. No one's ever looked at me the way he looks at me. I feel a silent rumble in my gut and I know something's just changed in me forever. I'll never be able to go back to comfortable and nice after feeling whatever it is burning between us. It scares the hell out of me and draws me in at the same time.

I watch as Nico closes his eyes and reopens them a few seconds later. I can see he's composing himself, and I feel weak that I don't have the strength to do the same. But I don't care. "Did you eat?"

I shake my head no. I went to a restaurant, but I never made it to dinner.

"Come on, I'll take you out to grab a bite." Although he doesn't release the hold he has on me. He watches me for a few seconds longer and then smiles down at me. "What is it about you, Elle?"

It's a question, but his face tells me he doesn't really expect an answer.

CHAPTER 12

Nico

"I think I wanna go back in." My words stop Preach in his tracks and he isn't prepared for the shot I land into his sparring gloves. He winds up on his ass.

I extend a hand down to him on the floor and he gets up rubbing his hip. "Do you think you can tell me this shit when I'm not going to get a bruise. A fucking cup of coffee. Maybe we sit down over a cup of coffee and discuss things like normal people for a change."

I shake my head at the drama of Preach. He's bugged the crap out of me for over a year and then he complains at the way I tell him I'm ready. Fucking Preach.

"Why the change of heart son?"

"Does it matter? You've been up my ass for a year and now I tell you what you've been wanting to hear and you start questioning it."

"How was your date last night?" A voice comes from behind me. I hadn't seen Lily walk in. I'm starting to regret hiring her to do my books. Her timing sucks and she's got a big mouth.

"The checkbook is upstairs." I don't respond to her question.

"Date?" Her comment gets Preach's attention.

"Oh, you haven't told Preach about Elle?" Lily drags out her words. She sounds like my sister teasing me. I'm suddenly glad that I grew up with three brothers who had no interest in gossip or my love life. I shoot Lily a look that says go away, but she stands her ground and her and Preach begin to talk about me like I'm not even there. She tells Preach about Elle and the two of them lap up the shit like two schoolgirls.

I'm stopped, waiting for Preach, and I feel my muscles starting to go cold. There's a pause in their chatter and I dart into the conversation before they can resume. "Think we can get back to work ladies? I'm not paying both your asses to stand around and talk about me like I'm not even here."

Lily smirks at Preach, but takes the hint and heads upstairs to get the books.

Preach lifts the pads he's holding to block my hits back up and I bounce up and down a few times to get the blood flowing again before I swing my leg high into the air and land a strong strike in the middle of the reflector pads, exactly where I aimed the kick.

"The girl have anything to do with your decision to get back into the cage?" Preach says as he repositions himself for the blow he thinks will come next.

I decide to change it up with a roundhouse that lands just barely on the reflector pads. He wasn't expecting another leg, and it catches him off guard, but he's able to recover and protect himself at the last minute.

I again ignore Preach's question about Elle. I don't even know if she likes MMA, so I'm not getting back into the cage to impress her, if that's what he thinks. The timing just feels right. I don't know why or what changed, I just feel ready today.

CHAPTER 13

Elle

"I can't believe you broke it off with William!" Regina claps her hands together in excitement as we tear into our lunch delivery. It's almost three and we are just getting around to eating. The day has been so busy. Leonard is due back next week and I'll be glad to go back to only dealing with my own caseload.

I'm surprised at Regina's excitement over my decision to end things with William. I always thought she liked him. "I thought you liked William?"

"I do dear. It's just. I don't know..." Regina trails off.

"Say it." I prompt her in a tone that tells her I really want to hear what she has to say.

"He's very nice, and handsome too."

"And?" I prompt.

"He's smart and polite."

"This doesn't sound like a list of the reasons that you would be happy I've stopped seeing someone." I pop a small cherry tomato into my mouth from my salad. "It sounds like the reasons you tell someone to start seeing them."

Regina smiles, but her face turns serious when she speaks. "I had twenty years with my husband, and I don't regret a minute of that time. He wasn't always polite, he didn't stand when I entered a room, he used foul language at the dinner table, but it was there."

I furrow my brow. I know she is trying to be helpful, but I'm not quite sure how any of what she is saying supports my breaking up with William.

Regina sees my confusion and continues. "But when he walked into a room, he took my breath away. He made my heart race and even after twenty years of marriage, I still wanted to rip his clothes off when he looked at me and I saw things in his eyes."

My mind goes to Nico. I feel those things about him. He makes my knees weak and tests my self-control like I've never endured before. I look up at Regina and see the pain fresh in her eyes. It's been more than ten years, but she still misses him like it happened yesterday. It saddens me to realize the strength of what she had and now it was gone.

I smile at Regina and nod in silence, letting her know I understand what she's trying to tell me.

"So let's get to the good stuff. When are you going out with Nico Hunter? That man looks at you like he wants to eat you alive." Regina wiggles her eyebrows suggestively. A look that she seems to use a lot when it comes to the subject of Nico Hunter.

I'm a little embarrassed to admit that I went directly from my break up with William to Nico's place last night, so I leave out some of the sordid details. "I saw him last night." My voice is low and sheepish.

"You dirty, dirty girl. I didn't think you had it in you!" Regina is teasing, I can see she's delighted at my news.

My face blushes as I think of what Nico looked like in his loft last night with no shirt on. He is quite possibly the most delectable thing I have ever laid eyes on. But I'm confused as to why he seems to put distance between us at certain times. Before we left to get dinner, I was sure that he was feeling what I felt. I could have sworn that I saw it in his eyes. There was desire there and I'm positive of it.

We had a great time at dinner too. There is no uncomfortable silence in our conversations and we both laughed through half of our meals. It's like we've known each other for years. Time goes by so quickly with him, the restaurant was almost empty when we finally realized it was time to leave. That's why I was a tangle of emotions when we got back to his place and he didn't try to get me to stay.

"We just went to dinner. Although I'll admit I was a little disappointed that he didn't try to get me to stay afterwards."

"I'm sure he was just being respectful Elle. Did you tell him you wanted to stay?"

"No."

Regina is about to respond when a deliveryman walks in carrying a huge bouquet of wildflowers. "Delivery for Elle James."

Neither one of us can wait until the deliveryman is out the door before I rip into the card with Regina peering over my shoulder. "Couldn't sleep all night thinking about you after you left."

Regina's smile beamed, as excited for me as I was. Truly a great friend.

CHAPTER 14

Elle

I leave work at five, instead of my usual seven or eight on Friday night so I have time to get ready for my date with Nico. I shave my legs and put on a matching lace bra and underwear set…just in case. Not that I'm planning on sleeping with him tonight, but I'd be kidding myself to think I'd stop it if things started to escalate. Nico Hunter might just be my kryptonite.

The buzzer rings and I feel like I'm fifteen again. The cute boy is about to talk to me and I swallow my words like an idiot and embarrass myself when I choke as I try to bring them back up. What the hell is wrong with me? I am smart and in control, and I'm acting like a complete idiot. I open the door and smile. Actually, I think I might have swooned instead of smiled. Do people actually swoon?

I step out of the way to allow Nico to enter. He takes one step inside and then turns to face me. My back is up against the door as he drops his head low to meet mine, brushing his lips softly against my mouth. "Hey."

"Hey." My response is breathless from just a whisper of his lips against mine.

Nico has mischief in his eyes that makes me want him to do things to me. It fuels my desire for his strong arms to pin me against the door and leave me powerless. It's not a feeling I'm familiar with, and it scares me to feel it as much as it excites me.

He enters my apartment and suddenly it feels smaller with such a massive man standing inside. "You cooked?"

"If you can call it that."

"It smells good." Nico crinkles up his nose and it is an absolutely adorable face. One that looks like he's five years old. I'm so enthralled by how such a large, powerful man can look so adorable, that it takes me a minute for his words to register. "But I think something is burning."

Smoke billows out of the oven when I open the door. I grab two oven mitts from behind me and pull out the salmon that fell victim to my incapable culinary hands. The pretty peachy-pink color is now brown on the top. I don't know how it could have burned so quickly, it had only been in there for less than half an hour.

Nico comes behind me and reaches to my side and turns the dial to the oven. "Bake, not broil."

Looking up at him, he can see that his words meant nothing to me, so he explains. "You needed to put the oven on bake, not broil."

Nico walks over to my refrigerator and opens the door to help himself. I see him grab something out of the cabinet, but I'm too busy trying to figure out how to salvage the mess I've made to pay any attention. He sets down a glass of wine he's poured me on the counter next to me and leans back against the counter in my U-shaped kitchen.

I lift the glass to my mouth and take a long sip before turning to face Nico, a few feet away from me. "I'm sorry, dinner is ruined."

Nico smiles at me and says nothing for a minute. "Come here," his voice is low and soft and he extends a thick arm to me. I comply and his arms wrap around my waist, gathering me close against his hard chest as he lowers his mouth to mine. Our lips connect and I follow his lead as his they open. His tongue slowly licks the outline of my lips, sending a shiver down my spine.

A low moan escapes my mouth and I feel his grip tighten in response. I surprise even myself when I bite down on his lower lip, drawing a low groan from him that makes what's between my legs swell with excitement. Nico tilts his head and our kiss deepens, our tongues explore each other's mouth with a passion I've never known or expected, yet it feels so natural and right.

We're both panting loudly when we come up for air. "I missed you." His voice is low and raspy. Sinful. It's only been two days since we saw each other, but I've missed him too.

"Me too." I manage to get out between breaths.

Nico's grip tightens on me almost to the point that it's painful, but I don't care. His hands are at my lower back and when he pulls me closer, I can feel his erection against my belly and I want to reach between us and grab him. Feel his thickness that is throbbing against me.

I think he's going to kiss me again, but instead he plants a soft kiss on the tip of my nose and then my forehead before engulfing me in a bear hug. It's such a tender moment and so unexpected after the passion of his kiss just a minute ago.

Too soon after, Nico loosens his grip on me.

"Where is your menu drawer?"

"How do you know I have a menu drawer?"

"I've seen how you cook first hand now, remember?"

Playfully, I smack at his stomach with the back of my hand and it meets a brick wall. "Second drawer down to the right of the sink."

Nico rummages through my menus. "You eat this junk?"

"Which one?" I look over at the pile of menus thinking he's found one that he doesn't approve of.

"All of them." For the first time, I look at my heap of menus and recognize that it's a pretty thick pile.

"Only when I want to eat." I smirk and Nico shakes his head disapprovingly, but I can tell he's teasing me. If I had a body that looked like his, I'd only feed it healthy food too. I might even learn to cook if I looked like him.

One menu catches his attention and seems to meet with his approval. "Is there anything you don't eat?"

"I'm pretty easy."

My response earns me a devilish grin before Nico takes out his cell phone and orders.

After we're done eating, Nico shows me the movie he brought and I look down at the movie, then at his face.

"Do you really want to watch this?"

The corner of his mouth twitches upward in barely concealed amusement. "Not really."

"Then why did you bring it?"

"I thought you'd like it?"

I tilt my hand to assess the man. He earns credit for bringing something that he thought I would like, but I'm not going to let him off this easy.

"Why?"

"Why what?"

"Why did you think I would like *The Notebook*?"

"Because you're a woman and women like this mushy crap."

Taking his hand, I lead him to my closet off the living room and open the door to reveal two shelves filled with some of my favorite movies. He peruses the titles and then looks back at me in shock, as if I had just showed him the dead body I kept locked in the closet instead of a simple movie collection.

"You like action movies?"

"The more jumping out of planes, the better."

Nico wraps his arm around my waist and turns me, pulling me to his chest before planting a chaste kiss on my mouth. He looks down at me. "Yep, totally worth it." I almost don't hear his words, they're spoken so low.

"Worth what?"

Another kiss is planted on my mouth. "Nothing."

Throughout the movie we have periodic make out sessions. Nico's big hands glide up and down the side of my body. His fingers slow as they pass the curve of my breasts and his thumb just barely grazes the swell underneath so that I can't be sure if his fingers touched me or just came really close.

As the movie credits roll on the screen, we're locked in a steamy kiss that I don't want to stop. My hands slowly feel their way down from his muscular chest and stop on his abdomen. I've never been the one to make the first move, but I don't care at this point. I want more from this man. Need more. My hands slip under his shirt and I gently score my nails against his tight flesh as my hands retrace their path down, stopping as I feel the top of his waistband.

A low growl erupts from Nico and he guides my back down on the couch as he climbs on top of me. With his weight pushing into me, I can feel every muscle up against mine and I swear I might finish before our naked flesh ever meets. He's just that damn incredible to feel. A low moan from somewhere within me escapes and our kissing becomes deeper, almost frantic.

Groaning, Nico sits up and leaves me breathless on the couch. My body is desperate and I need more. When I look up, I find Nico running his hands through his hair in frustration.

"Why did you stop?" My voice comes out like a whiney high school girl who is unsure of herself with her new boyfriend. But that's what the man has reduced me to, heavy panting and desire with no happy ending.

"You have no idea how hard it is to stop." His voice is raw and honest and filled with emotion. Somehow it makes me feel better knowing it isn't easy for him. But it also confuses me. Why does he keep stopping?

"So why then?"

Nico struggles for a moment, "Because I want you to know me first, so I don't scare you away."

"Why would you scare me away?"

He thinks for a long moment, before he responds. "Because it's who I am." Nico looks at me and touches the side of my face gently with his thumb. "You're a beautiful, smart, strong woman who is used to being treated like a lady."

I'm confused at his words and Nico sees it on my face. He pulls me to him and buries his face in my neck. His breath is so close to my ear when he speaks, I feel the words throughout my body as he speaks them. "But when I finally get you underneath me, I'm definitely not going to treat you like a lady."

CHAPTER 15

Elle

Regina buzzes in to tell me William is on the phone. It's the first time I've heard from him since I told him I couldn't see him anymore. When I told him I wanted to remain friends, it wasn't just a line. Our friendship is important to me, and I'm glad he called, although I hadn't expected to hear from him so soon.

"Hi."

"Hey." A second too long goes by that makes me feel like this might be an awkward conversation.

"I wanted to let you know that your letter was a success." William's tone is more business than friendship.

Momentarily, I'm not following the conversation. Then I realize what he must be referring to. "They're going to let Nico out of the contract?"

"Yes, they seem to agree with you that it's in their best interest to walk away rather than entertain a public lawsuit regarding their ethics." My letter was a bit more underhanded than I normally would like. A thinly disguised, veiled threat to remind them we didn't even have to be successful in a lawsuit over their ethics. The damage to their reputation would come through public persona, just from trying the case in a public forum.

"That's great news. Have you told Nico yet?" My voice comes out a little more excited than I had intended it to.

"No. I called you first. If you want to call him and give him the good news, that's okay with me."

Briefly, I feel badly about wanting to be the one who tells Nico the good news. But another part of me wants to be the one that pleases him. William tells me he will fax over the termination paperwork for my review and I agree to look at it as soon as it comes over since they want a response quickly.

After we hang up, I realize just how clinical our conversation was and I feel badly that our friendship may not make it.

CHAPTER 16

Nico

I easily knock the first two guys Preach puts in the ring with me on their asses. He's trying to build my confidence, but I'm losing patience. "Give me a real partner or I'm done for the day."

Preach laughs at me. "They are real partners, you just got a bug up your ass today. But let's keep it there for the next three weeks."

It takes less than three minutes to blow through the third sparring partner, and I feel more frustrated than when I started. Preach is blowing smoke up my ass about how good I look, but I think he's just giving me weak partners.

I spend the next fifteen minutes taking what the jerkoffs in the ring couldn't handle out on the speed bag. My knuckles are swollen and bloodied by the time I've let off enough steam to take a calm breath.

Preach looks at my knuckles and shakes his head. We've been together too long for him not to recognize when something is bothering me. Sometimes he knows what it is before I do.

"What's eating you son?"

"Nothing."

"Alright. How's things going with Elle?"

"Great." I pick up the jump rope and begin to swing it at warp speed. The rope slips under my feet twice with each hop.

"Preach." I lower my voice so none of the gym rats can hear me. "How long do normal people date before they sleep together?"

Preach laughs. He thinks I'm kidding.

"No really, how long?"

"Is that what this is about? You're hard up?" Preach laughs and I get the urge to whip his ass with the rope that I can't seem to stop swinging. I have so much pent up energy, it feels like I could workout for days and still be raring to go.

"That's right, you're used to the girls just dropping their panties at your feet before you open that foul mouth of yours." Preach laughs. "You finally found one that's making you work for it?"

Sal, the guy working the front desk today, whistles to get my attention. "Phone for you."

"Tell whoever it is, I'm working out and I'll call him back." I look at Sal like he's lost his mind for interrupting my workout for a phone call.

"Okay, but it's a woman."

I hear Preach and Sal snickering on my way to the phone.

CHAPTER 17

Elle

Hearing his voice on the phone makes me smile. I tell Nico the good news and offer to drop off the documents for him to review on my way to my three o'clock appointment. He promises unhealthy takeout for me in exchange for my time. His version of unhealthy and my version are vastly different, but I'm anxious to see him again anyway.

Traffic is much lighter than usual, and I'm early when I arrive at Nico's gym. Early. I never get anywhere early, even if there are no cars on the road I'm usually late. The guy at the door eyes me suspiciously as I enter, he probably thinks I'm entering the wrong building. The red suit I'm wearing is one of my favorites. It pinches in at the waist and emphasizes my curves in all the right places. But I'm definitely overdressed for a gym.

"I have a feeling you're in the wrong place, but I'm glad you came in because I think I've fallen in love." His line may be all wrong, but his smile is friendly so I smile back innocently.

Nico smacks the guy in the back of the head, but I can tell he doesn't really want to hurt him. "You got one warning Sal. Keep your comments and your eyes to yourself, or you won't make it into the ring the next time I kick your ass."

Nico walks around the front desk and puts his arm around my waist and pulls me to him protectively before kissing me sweetly on the lips.

Sal snickers as he rubs the back of his head and mutters something about Nico having all the luck.

His hand on the small of my back, Nico guides me through the gym. I'm not sure if women just don't come in the place often, or if seeing me with Nico has thrown people, but I notice everyone stop what they're doing as we make our way to an office in the back of the gym.

A man is sitting behind the desk typing on a keyboard with one finger. Pecking would be a more appropriate description. He looks up and sits back in the chair, a knowing smile on his face.

"Preach, this is Elle."

"Hiya Elle. I've heard a lot about you." The man stands and extends his hand to me, a warm smile on his face. I like him instantly, but I'm not sure why, I just do.

I look from Preach to Nico, raising an eyebrow in question to Nico, silently asking him what the man may have heard about me.

"I guess I should be thanking you." Preach says with my hand still wrapped in his as he continues to shake my hand for longer than a normal handshake.

"You can let go of her hand now, Preach." Nico tries to sound threatening, but it's obvious that the two men respect each other and the banter is something that they're both used to.

Nico tells Preach that I was able to get him out of the contract and Preach looks impressed. On his way out the door, Preach smacks Nico on the back. "Smart and beautiful. So what the hell is she doing with a schlep like you?"

Nico laughs off the comment and shuts the door behind him. I watch as he locks the door before turning to me with a devilish grin on his face.

Without speaking, he places his hands on my waist and easily lifts me, positioning me on top of his desk. The look in his eyes makes my body tingle all over. He takes one large hand and wraps it around the back of my head, holding it in place where he wants it. I wait while he leans down and covers my mouth with his. It's not a hello kiss. It's a kiss that makes me feel like he wants to mark me. Like he needs to show me that no one else will come after him.

Uncaring that I'm wearing a skirt, I wrap my legs around his waist as he leans into me further. The sheer fabric on my lace panties does little to dull the sensation of his hardness pushing into my most sensitive area. His other arm reaches around to my ass and pulls me into him. Hard. Already pressed up against him, the additional pressure acts as a trigger and sends a bolt of electricity between my legs where I'm already swollen. The smallest amount of friction might help me find my release that I've so desperately needed since I met this man.

I nip at his lower lip when he attempts to take his mouth away from me. Nico groans and responds by squeezing a huge chunk of flesh on my ass that he is already holding snugly. It's just shy of painful, but falls on the other side. The side where the groping and grabbing is erotic and it ratchets up my need to new levels.

A knock at the door brings me crashing down to reality. On my way down I see myself propped on the edge of a desk in my suit with my legs parted panting like a wild animal. Throwing a bucket of cold water over my head would only have had a lesser effect on my libido. Whoever is on the other side of the door, doesn't take the hint when no one responds, which only fuels their curiosity and the knock becomes painstakingly louder.

"I'm going to kill whoever is on the other side of that door." Nico leans his forehead against mine, and it helps my initial embarrassment to know he's as affected as I am.

He kisses me once more on the lips. "Don't move an inch." Something about the tone of his voice sounds more like a command and for once I want to listen instead of challenge the authority that speaks.

Nico walks to the door and cracks it open. I'm still sitting on the edge of the desk. Surprising even myself that I haven't jumped up to regain my composure.

"Preach told me not to knock, but I have to pick up my little sister in an hour and I didn't want to run out of time." A young boy's voice unnerves me as I sit completely disheveled with my skirt up around my ass just a few feet away from the door. I jump up and frantically begin to fix myself. Nico catches me out of the corner of his eye and I see his jaw clench.

"You're gonna run an extra mile for not listening to Preach. Go give me six on the treadmill and if I'm done in here we'll see how much time is left."

I hear the boy whine, but seconds later his footsteps tell me he listened.

Nico shuts the door and turns his attention back to me. I've already righted my clothing and I'm no longer sitting on the desk. "You weren't supposed to move."

"There was a little boy five feet away and my underwear was showing." I cross my arms, letting him know he can expect that this isn't a one-time occurrence. Listening isn't always my strong suit.

He shakes his head from side to side but his head is down and I can't see his face to read what he's feeling. Standing my ground, I don't move from my spot as he walks back to me, completely invading my personal space. He looks down at me, his eyes are still half-mast from our encounter and I gulp finding my mouth suddenly dry from the way he's looking at me. "Saturday night. I'll make you dinner." He looks up at me to gauge my reaction. "Bring a bag because I'm not letting you go next time."

The swell between my legs that was ebbing, flows back at a rapid pace. "Okay." My voice cracks as I respond with a whisper.

Nico lifts my chin, forcing me to look into his eyes. "Okay?" Even though he told me what I was doing this weekend, he still wants confirmation.

My eyes don't waiver as I respond. I force my voice louder. "Okay."

Nico smiles like I've just given him a prize he really wanted, and it's contagious. Mirroring his enthusiasm, I can't help but smile back.

He takes my hand and grabs my bag and another bag that I'm all too familiar with. Take out.

His hand reaches for the door and he pauses. "We can't eat in here or I can't promise I will control myself. You look so damn sexy in that suit and the way you smell makes me lose control."

We eat our lunch in a small lunchroom that's open to the gym and I walk Nico through the main points of the contract termination I've brought him. He's forgoing a multi-million dollar endorsement payout and has to give back a substantial amount of money he's already been advanced. If it bothers him at all, he does a good job not letting it show.

CHAPTER 18

Elle

Saturday morning I call my mom to check in. I feel guilty I don't call often enough, but sometimes I just need to try to block out that part of my life. It's not my mom's fault that I can't separate her from the past that haunts me. I don't mean to, but so much is deeply interwoven that it's hard to take the good out from a web of bad memories.

Four years of therapy helped me to start to live again, and these days I really think I'm doing it. Guilt for not feeling regret had me stuck in a bad place, but most days I think I've moved on. Most days.

Mom and I spend ten minutes catching up and then the conversation moves to William. She casually asks how he is and is surprised when I tell her that we recently stopped seeing each other. I don't mention that I've started seeing someone because I'm not in the mood for the third degree. Not today. I wouldn't lie to her if she asked, but I know she would ask whether I've shared my past with him or not. For some reason she seems to think that telling people about the worst day of my life is cathartic. Perhaps it would be, but I wouldn't know since I've never told a living soul outside of my weekly group meetings. Sure, lots of people know. But those are the people that read the headlines. They didn't hear it from my lips.

After I hang up, I spend an hour trying to figure out what to wear to Nico's. The outside layer of clothing is the easy part. But I want to look sexy without my clothes on. It dawns on me that I've never been concerned over what I wore for William. Not even in the beginning. Perhaps I should have been, but there's no use dwelling on that now. Whatever the reason, I feel the need to please Nico Hunter. I've never felt that way with another man. A few weeks ago, if a woman would have told me that she dressed to please her man, I probably would have thought she was pitiful. But the way that Nico looks at me makes me high. It's like a drug I crave desperately to have again. His pleasure is my reward, and I'm willing to do whatever it takes to earn it.

I'm honest with myself about how I feel, but it doesn't make me accept my own reaction to the man any easier. I'm torn between giving in to what feels so right and chastising myself for acting like a weak little girl.

I manage to get a few hours of work in during the afternoon. My workweek is always six days, but with Leonard out it's pushing seven. A half day today and possibly no work tomorrow will make my Monday brutal, but I'll care about that Monday.

I arrive at his building on time. The only two times I've been on time to anything in the last year have both involved Nico Hunter. Even I can't chalk that up to coincidence. As I make my way to the door, I'm nervous and fidgety. Anticipation wreaks havoc on my ability to multitask and I don't even notice he's standing in the doorway, as I fumble in my purse to put away my keys while walking.

"Hey, beautiful." His voice is low and sexy, but it scares the shit out of me nonetheless, because I hadn't realized anyone was there.

I jump and look up, spilling the contents of my overly stuffed purse all over the concrete.

"I'm sorry, I didn't mean to scare you. I thought you saw me standing there."

Nico leans down to start cleaning up the mess, and I almost lose my balance in my heels as I lower myself to join him in collecting my things. He smiles at me with a sexy smile and I smile back. I'm momentarily lost in his knee weakening smile, until I see what he's holding in his hand out of the corner of my eye and realize it's the reason for his sly smile. My birth control pills. He extends his hand to offer them to me, but doesn't release them as I go to take them.

"Good to know." Nico's smile has grown from a smirk to a full-blown, panty-dropping grin and I feel the red creep up over my face. God damn it, I'm a grown woman who accepted an invitation to stay at a man's house tonight, but yet I blush at the site of birth control pills. What the hell is wrong with me?

I quickly scoop up the rest of my personal life on display on the sidewalk and I'm relieved that I had removed the flavored condoms that Regina had shoved into my purse before I left yesterday. Bacon flavor. What woman wants to taste meat while, you know, tasting meat?

Nico stands and doesn't offer to help me get up. He just does it. After I'm balanced he leans in and plants a soft kiss on my lips. Not much more than a brush, but I feel it all the way down to my toes. And we are standing in the middle of the sidewalk. There aren't any people around, but still, it's out of character for me to have a public display of affection. Or at least it was before.

"You didn't bring a bag?" Nico's face looks so disappointed, like a little boy who was just told he couldn't have the puppy he'd been planning on bringing home.

"I did, I just left it in the car." Nico tilts his head and squints his eyes at me.

"You're not sure if you want to stay?" I can hear the disappointment in his voice.

"Umm." How do I respond to him? Of course I want to stay, but it felt funny walking into his house with an overnight bag, even though he invited me. Almost presumptuous.

Nico takes my hesitation as confirmation that I'm not sure if I want to stay. He takes a step forward and wraps one arm around my waist, resting just north of my ass. The other hand moves to behind my head and he kisses me. Fiercely. His tongue seeks mine, then he sucks on the tip of it as he pulls it away to add teeth. His teeth bite down on my bottom lip and just as I begin to feel the pain from his bite, he sucks and licks away at the spot he just wounded, making it more than better.

I feel his hand that was holding my lower waist travel down and he pulls me flush against him tightly as his hands roam over my ass and he cups almost my whole cheek in one large palm. Tingling sensations shoot through my veins and I feel the sensitive skin between my legs swell. Nico growls and squeezes me harder before he pulls back slightly, releasing my mouth, tugging at my lip between his teeth as he pulls away.

I have no idea where I am. My senses are all keenly focused on the man who just stole my breath and I'm panting when he finally releases my mouth fully. His breath is fast as his mouth drops to my ear and he speaks in a strained voice. "I'm about ten seconds away from losing my self-control, Babe. Think I can get that bag for you and move this inside so we don't give the whole neighborhood a show?"

Nico pulls his head back and waits for my answer. But I can't speak yet, so I nod my head yes and just watch as he takes my keys out of my hand. He kisses me again on the mouth, this time much softer. "Not that I would mind. I don't give a shit who's watching as long as I get to do that to you."

I force myself to close my mouth as I stand there watching him grab my bag from the car and return to me, his disappointed face now replaced with a megawatt smile that reminds me of his fighting name. Lady Killer. If the name fits…

Inside, things cool down, which I'm grateful for. Or, at the rate I was going on the street, I would have been in his bed within fifteen minutes of my arrival. Nico picks me up and seats me on the kitchen island, so we can talk while he cooks. Watching him breeze around his kitchen, I realize how sexy a man who knows his way around the kitchen can be. There's something instinctually alluring about a man who wants to take care of his woman. Not that I'm the barefoot-and-pregnant-in-the-kitchen-type of woman. But this is different. An almost natural role that he takes in our relationship and I find that I like to be taken care of. It's something I have never allowed anyone to do before.

CHAPTER 19

Nico

I need to slow things down. I almost took her on the street for fuck's sake. I feel like I'm stuck in a bad movie, with a little devil sitting on one shoulder and an angel on the other. But the goddamn devil is twice the size and my angel is a fucking mute. Great, I have a fucking mute angel.

She looks so cute up on the counter, I get the urge to bring her with me wherever I go and just plop her up on a pedestal near me. But as I grab a bottle of water out of the refrigerator, I see her reflection in the stainless steel. She crosses and recrosses her legs and I catch a glimpse of the top of her thigh for a split second. Damn it, I can feel myself starting to get hard from a damn reflection of a thigh. Freakin mute angel. Think thoughts of my grandmother. Grandmother Ellen. Ellen, hey that's just Elle with an n. Elle's legs. Shit this isn't working.

"That smells good. What are you making?" I turn my head to respond to her, but it takes a minute for her question to catch up to my brain.

Not half as good as you smell. I'd like to eat you instead. "Couscous."

"You make couscous?"

"Well it doesn't taste good straight from the box."

"Cute." She smirks at me. Even her smirk turns me on. "What's in it?"

"Garlic, olive oil, peppers, onions, parsley…"

Elle jumps down from the counter. I had put her there to keep her at a distance. She doesn't realize what she does to me every time she comes near me.

"Can I help?" Her arm brushes against mine as she comes to stand next to me at the counter. She leans down over the pan where the ingredients are sautéing and her eyes close as she breathes in the aroma. Clearly, she appreciates the smell. Her face softens and her cheeks go slack as her nose delivers the scent to her brain. It's the most erotic thing I've ever seen. She needs to get back up on that fucking counter.

CHAPTER 20

Elle

Nico lifts me as if I am nothing but a doll and seats me back on the counter. It's the second time he's moved me out of the way. The man sure is territorial about his kitchen when he cooks, oddly, I find it sexy. The inside of his hand brushes the curve of my breast each time he lifts me and I have to recross my legs and squeeze my thighs shut to keep my body from responding to him.

"I've seen you cook, remember? I think I'll do this one on my own." He grins at me. A cocky smile that should annoy me. But instead I find myself mirroring his smile. I'm smiling back at him after he just insulted me. The man makes me lose all my common sense.

Dinner is delicious. We get to know each other a little more. I tell him about my job, my volunteer work at the battered women's clinic, and a few things about my childhood. I skip between the ages of eleven and seventeen. They don't exist to me anymore. Nico tells me about his gym and some of the other products he endorses and I'm impressed by how much he seems to know about the products. Clearly he doesn't endorse something unless he uses it and feels strongly about it. Unlike many athletes that endorse one product and use another, money doesn't seem to buy his endorsement.

After dinner, I tell him to go relax and let me clean up. He doesn't listen, so instead we do it together. It feels natural and comfortable to clean up his kitchen. We work together easily, without effort...

like we've done it a thousand times before. It's not the first time I've gotten that feeling when I'm with Nico. Sometimes I feel as though I've known him a lot longer than I have. Oddly familiar, yet it's all new and exciting at the same time.

My heartbeat picks up as Nico pours me a glass of wine and dims the lights in the kitchen. With dinner out of the way, there's nothing left to occupy our time. Except what I think we're both anticipating will happen. We haven't known each other that long, yet I feel like I've been anticipating this night forever. Since the day he walked into my office.

He takes my hand and leads me to the couch. Nico looks up at me and his cocky grin is gone, replaced by something that I didn't expect to see written on his face. He looks worried. He exhales loudly, forcing out a deep breath I didn't realize he was holding, and his hands run through his hair nervously. It feels like he's mentally preparing himself to tell me something. To deliver bad news. My stomach lurches at the thought.

"Have you ever been to a fight?" The loft is quiet and his voice is so low it sounds almost pained.

"You mean an MMA fight?"

"Yes." He waits quietly for my response.

"Once."

Nico's eyebrows shoot up. He's surprised that I've been to a fight. I grin at him. He's right to be surprised, I still can't believe I got conned into going. I haven't told him that I was at one of his fights. Especially not the one that I saw. He smiles back at me, but then his face falls again before he continues.

"Who was fighting?"

"You." It's not like the subject has come up in our conversation and I lied to him, yet I feel like I've done something wrong for not mentioning that I was at a fight. *That* fight.

My answer takes him my surprise. "You've seen me fight?"

"Once."

84

"Which fight?"

"I don't remember the other guy's name." I should remember, I remember everything. But I'm not lying when I respond. I've blocked the whole thing from my memory so well that I actually don't remember. I'm good at doing that. Luckily, my brain goes into protective mode sometimes.

"Did I win?" I see a hint of his cocky smile. He must have always won.

"Yes." I smile.

"Did he tap out or was it a decision?"

"Ummm." I have no idea how to respond to the question. Nico probably thinks I don't know what tap out means. But I do. Only in that fight, his opponent didn't tap out and there was no need for a decision.

"What round did I win in?"

"I think it was the second."

I watch as his face changes. His eyes close as he realizes which fight I saw. His handsome face is pained and I'm not sure if it's the memory of that night or if it's because I've just told him I was there. I say nothing because I'm not sure what to say. I only know that seeing him in pain hurts me. Physically.

I reach out and take both of his hands into my hands and gently squeeze, imploring him to look at me. He doesn't move for a long moment. His head still bowed down, he eventually looks up at me. What I see breaks my heart. Raw pain in his eyes and sadness etched on his face.

"You know." His voice is strained and I get the urge to make it better. Make him better. Make him forget the memory that causes him so much pain. Sometimes it can be unbearable, I know all too well. All those years I had no one to help me forget.

I nod my head once. His words weren't a question, but I gave him the answer anyway. I watch as Nico closes his eyes for a long moment before looking back at me. Something hits him and I'm not sure what it is, but some of the pain that was there a minute ago flees from his face. Some of it is still there, but it's less pronounced now.

"You're here anyway." His face is so serious and intent. It's such an odd, surreal moment. His eyes are locked with mine, filled with intensity and pain and everything in the background falls away. There is nothing in the moment except me and Nico. The here and now, everything else is just a blur because he holds my sole focus.

I don't even know where my response comes from. I'm a think before you speak type of person. But I hold his gaze as the words fall from my lips, time stops for my simple five word response and when it starts back up again, everything is different. "Where else would I be?" My words are spoken softly, but they connect with Nico instantly.

For a split second I see something in his eyes that I can't place, but it warms me all over. Like being wrapped in a warm blanket when you're cold, it brings me comfort and heat and I just want to crawl under and stay there. Nico is silent as he stands. I look up just as he reaches down and scoops me up into his big arms. He cradles me tightly as he walks. Neither of us say a word, we just watch each other.

We enter what must be his bedroom and he gently sets me down in the middle of his big bed. But he doesn't join me right away. Instead he stands up and takes it all in. Me, laying in the middle of his bed. I think he's taking a mental picture, as if he wants to sear it into his brain and remember it forever. It makes me feel adored. It's the sweetest thing a man has ever done and it took no words.

His long, slow, heated gaze sweeps up my body and when his eyes finally reach my eyes, I can barely take the wait anymore. I want him. So damn badly. It's actually more of a need than a want. It should scare me to feel what I'm feeling, but it doesn't. There is no room for scared between us. I reach up and offer him my hand, and Nico looks between my eyes and my hand and back again before taking it. The silent confirmation of what I need is enough and I finally get what I want.

Slowly, he half covers my body with his, the other half of his weight supported by the bed. The part that is touching me is thick and hard and I wish that his body was completely over mine so I could feel each and every rippled muscle pressed against me. Instead, he uses the space between us to brush his big hand over the side of my body.

His hand starts at the middle of my thigh and painstakingly slowly runs up my side. Nico's eyes don't leave mine as his hand travels. When his hand reaches the side of my breast, his thumb gently reaches out and feels the curve of my swell. A small gasp escapes me, it's small, but Nico catches it and I can actually see the green in his eyes darken at my response. He's watching me, taking in my every reaction to his touch and I get the sense that he's as aroused as I am from his simple touch.

My eyes close when his hand reaches my face. He softly caresses my cheek with his calloused thumb. Gentle, soft, barely a brush. His tender touch makes me feel worshipped and I try to fight back emotion from flooding. It's my instinct, but it's a losing battle. One I never surrendered to until now.

I open my eyes and watch as Nico's eyes drop to my mouth and back again. His head leans down and I think he is finally going to kiss me, but instead he buries his head in my neck and breathes deep, scenting me. He lets out a low growl as he exhales and I swear it makes every hair on my body stand upright. It's as if an electric current ran from the top of my head to the tips of my toes and I'm frayed from the bolt that shot through me.

Nico draws his head back from my neck and his eyes take mine again. He's so close to me now, I can't help but reach up and touch him. My pointer finger slowly comes up and I trace his beautiful full lips with a gentle touch, slowly, etching their shape into my memory. His mouth parts and he takes a deep breath before closing his eyes. I can see he's straining for control when he reopens them a few seconds later.

It's incredibly sexy to watch such a strong man so close to losing control. It fuels my need to push him. Push him over the edge of restraint, where his control disappears and the feral male I see lurking beneath takes control. I want to see what it will take to get him there.

After I'm done tracing his lips, I push my finger into his mouth. It's warm and wet and he takes my invitation. I watch as he gently suckles on my finger at first. I bite down on my own bottom lip as his sucking gets stronger. My eyes tear away from his mouth to find his eyes and he's still watching me. Watching me watch him. I see a glint in his eye and I catch the corner of his mouth turning upward in a smirk just before he bites down on my finger. Hard. Pain shoots through me mixed with need and desire, and I'm momentarily stunned at his action.

Nico releases my finger and I think I hear him say, "There's the fire," and then he's on me. His mouth covers mine and we fuse together. It's a desperate kiss, all tongue and slippery, with sucking and biting. One that consumes me the moment it starts and I instantly need more.

My hips mindlessly push up into him and I'm met with hardness. Thick, long, rock-solid hardness. My body trembles at the feel of his arousal so closely against me and another low moan escapes me. I don't think I've ever moaned uncontrollably, but now it pours from a deep place within me. Nico tries to pull his head back, but I wrap my arms tighter around his neck and keep him where I need him.

He manages to free himself from my death grip and pulls his head back slightly. I am just about to complain when he says, "I need to taste all of you." I seriously think I have a mini orgasm at his words. The thought of his head between my legs sends a wicked shiver down my spine and I wiggle as Nico lifts his weight off me and settles with his head between my thighs.

I forget we're both still completely dressed until Nico pushes up my skirt and his mouth covers me, my lace underwear still between us. I feel the warmth of his mouth and his rapid breath up against my most sensitive skin and it's torment. The need to have nothing between us is overwhelming and I'm just about to beg when I feel the heat of his mouth leave me. Nico gently removes my skirt and underwear and I brace for an explosion. But then he's still. After a few seconds I look down and he's looking up at me, waiting to catch my eye before he speaks. His voice is low and gruff, but filled with blatant desire. "I want you to watch."

My body begins to spasm on its own at his words. I can't respond, but I don't look away either. Nico slowly draws out his tongue and licks me unhurriedly from my entrance to my clit. He stops as he reaches my swollen bundle of nerves and flitters his tongue ever so slightly over it. I whimper at his gentle touch, but I need more. More friction, more tongue, more suction. Just more. I lift my hips up in search of the more I quiver to find and Nico flashes me a knowing grin. He knows exactly what he's doing to me. Any embarrassment I feel from needing more goes out the window when I realize he's teasing me and I tangle my fingers into his hair and push his face down into me, desperately seeking the friction I need.

Nico's mouth claims me. He circles my clit around and around before sucking hard, taking my swell into his mouth and lashing me with his wicked tongue. There is no build to my orgasm, no warning. Just a hard, heart pounding, endless wave of pulsating orgasm that tears through me violently. So violently I feel tears well up in my eyes for no reason other than pure emotion and euphoria needs to escape from where it's trapped inside of my body.

I'm so completely spent from the intensity of what just happened that I barely participate in the next few minutes of frantic activity. Nico has to undress us both. I hear the foil wrapper opening, but it's his words that bring me back to the current. "Last chance to say no, Elle."

After all that he's said and done to me, he's still giving me an out. I feel my heart tug in my chest, adoring that he is still putting my needs before his own. Because of it, I want him that much more. "I can't remember ever wanting anything more than I want you right now." I look into his beautiful green eyes as I speak, letting him see through to the vulnerability that I'd kept locked away for so long.

He responds to my declaration with a kiss. Calling it a kiss just doesn't seem like enough, it's so much more. But there's no name for two people becoming so entangled in each other that they get lost. For wanting someone so badly that your body trembles waiting for more. So much more.

I feel his swollen head at my opening and he breaks our kiss. The moment he draws his head back from me, I crave his lips back on mine. But he wants to watch me as he enters me for the first time. I find it arousing and erotic, and I find myself wanting to show him what he is doing to me, instead of hiding my emotions. It's so unlike me.

I've felt his hardness between us, so I know he's large, but I never fully felt him to know exactly how big he is. Until he's pushing inside of me. He's gentle, like he knows he can't give it to me all at once, that he might tear me in half if he rams into me too quickly. He eases into me and stills, allowing my body to accommodate his thick girth. His hips make small, gentle circles, enabling my body to stretch before he pushes the rest of the way in. He moves slowly and I keep thinking that he must be all the way in, but then he keeps on inching in. Inch after inch of glorious thickness that fills me to the max. By the time the base of his thick cock hits against my body, I'm starting to worry I won't be able to take anymore. But he settles and begins to swivel his hips gently, grinding his perfect body slowly up and down, each time brushing my clit, sending a jolt through my body.

Nico looks down into my eyes and I feel full. Incredibly full. But not just from his thick length slowly rocking into me, I'm full of so much more. Emotion, warmth, raw feeling. Something I haven't felt in a very long time. Alive.

My eyes start to close as I feel my next orgasm rise to the surface. I want to let it wash over me, surrender to its intensity. But Nico has other plans. He gently kisses my lips and whispers to me, "I want to watch you. Please." His words are so tender and soft, I'm unable to deny him anything. My orgasm rolls over me and I fight the urge to close my eyes. Instead I keep Nico's gaze and give him what he wants, allowing him to feel my orgasm through my eyes as my body milks him through waves of uncontrolled spasms.

I'm shaking as he comes. His hips finally changing from a soft thrust to a ferocious pounding. I feel his thickness growing inside of me and then he comes on a growl. A raw, primal growl that is so intensely sensual that it detonates an unexpected orgasm from my body and we both pant through our climax together. It's the most powerful intimate experience of my entire life, and it's only our first time together.

I don't remember falling asleep, but I wake up before Nico. I can tell it's morning by the light straining to come in through the drawn window shade. My head is resting in the crook of his shoulder and his grip is tight around me, even in his sleep. I admire the beautiful man holding me, his muscles bulging even in his relaxed state. It's crazy how perfect his body is, as if it was sculpted by an artist. And the tattoos. Damn, the tattoos just add to the beauty, making him look like an exotic creature. I've never been with a man with tattoos. I've liked them from afar, but never had one in my bed. Men with this many tattoos tend to have an edge. A bad boy. I only go for the safe ones. At least I did.

Although I'm thoroughly enjoying watching him sleep, I need to go to the bathroom. I carefully untangle myself from Nico's thick arms, cautiously trying not to wake him. I spend a few minutes in the bathroom cleaning myself up and running my fingers through my hair. I look in the mirror and realize I look different, but I'm not sure what it is that I see to make me feel that way. Relaxed perhaps?

I make it back to the bed and I think I've succeeded at not waking him, when a large arm grabs me and I'm suddenly on my back beneath Nico. It's a little unnerving the way he tosses me around like I'm light as a feather, but at the same time I find it incredibly sexy. "Good morning, beautiful." Nico buries his head in my neck as he speaks. His words vibrate with heat on my neck and goose bumps break out all over my body.

I can't see his face, but I hear in his voice that he's smiling. I smile back at him even though he can't see me either. "Good morning." I lift my chin, giving him better access to the spot he's gently sucking and I feel his arousal on my leg. He's hard and it's not just the erection that men seem to wake up with.

Nico shifts his hips and his body completely covers mine, I feel him positioned perfectly at my opening. But he pauses and pulls his head back to look at me. "Are you sore?"

I actually am pretty sore. And not just my private area. My whole body feels a little beat up from the night before. But it's a good feeling and I want more of him. I attempt to minimize my discomfort, knowing full disclosure might lead to him stopping. "Not really."

Nico drops his head and I hear a deep chuckle. "You know, for a lawyer, you're a shit liar."

"Are you saying that lawyers are usually good liars?"

Nico arches an eyebrow in amusement. "That's what I'm saying."

"And how do you know that I'm lying? Maybe I'm not sore. Maybe you're just too full of yourself thinking that you can make me sore that easily."

Both of Nico's eyebrows shoot up in response to my comment. "Well for starters, I asked you a direct question and you responded *not really*. I seem to remember that's what you say when you have an answer that I'm not going to like."

I squint my eyes and furrow my brows in an effort to look pissed off. But there's no use. He's absolutely right and I can't pretend he's not. I let out an exasperated, over exaggerated sigh and roll my eyes. "So maybe I'm a little sore."

Nico smirks, looking full of himself. I'm not sure if he's full of himself for being right or for making me sore. Both would be my guess. But then something in his face changes and I watch his eyes darken before he begins to climb off of me. I reach for him as his body is half lifted off of mine. "Where are you going?"

"I'm hungry. I was going to have some breakfast since you're sore."

I begin to answer, ready to argue with him, when I realize what he's doing. He isn't lifting himself off of me, he's lowering himself down my body. Nico is hungry and I can't wait to be his meal.

CHAPTER 21

Nico

Elle walks into the kitchen wearing nothing but the button up shirt I was wearing last night and a satisfied smile. I feel like fucking Tarzan and it takes everything I have not to bang on my chest, knowing I put that satisfaction on her face. Again.

She looks sexy as hell and I need back inside of her. Soon. I can't remember the last time I made a woman breakfast. The last thirteen months I've treated women like stray cats. I'd pet em a bit, but if I fed them and they knew where I lived, I was afraid they'd come back. But Elle's different. I want her to stay. I want to make her breakfast and then spend the day with her, maybe even spend some of the day outside of bed.

She's quiet and I hope she isn't thinking of how to make her getaway. She tries to steal a piece of turkey bacon I'm making, and I swat her ass with the spatula. Hmm. I hope she stays, so we can play with the spatula more. I toss her up onto the island, her bare legs swing around reminding me of a little kid. She's smart and sexy and cute and has no idea of it.

"You have any plans for the day?" I'm venturing into uncharted territory here. It's usually the other way around. They want to stay and I can't wait to get rid of them.

"Umm. None that I really want to do. I have some work to catch up on, but it'll keep."

I take a piece of bacon over to her and feed it to her. She doesn't attempt to take it from my hand. Instead she sits on the counter and bites off pieces. She smiles at me as she takes the last piece in her mouth, nipping my finger on purpose. The woman doesn't have an ounce of fear of me, even knowing what I'm capable of.

She lifts her eyebrow at me in challenge after her nip. "What do you normally do on Sundays?"

"I usually wind up downstairs, even though I tell myself I'm not going to work." I take another piece of bacon from the plate over to her and offer her one bite. As she chews I pull her ass almost off the counter so she is flush up against me. The height is perfect. I'm definitely taking her in the kitchen like this when she isn't sore. I pretend to offer her another bite of bacon, and then pull it back, shoving the rest of the piece into my own mouth instead.

She playfully pouts and shoves at me, but I don't budge. "Preach and I also usually have dinner with Vinny Sunday night."

"Vinny?"

"He's a local kid I train. Mom's a fu…screw up and he was on his way to a bad place. Got in trouble for fighting at school all the time, so I'm working on giving him focus. He's a good kid, but don't ever tell him I said that."

"Your secret's safe with me. I won't let on that you're really a good guy."

I wrap my arms around her waist. "You better not, I have a reputation to live up to, you know." I plant one on her lips before finishing off our breakfast.

CHAPTER 22

Elle

"Oh my god, this is so good. What did you put in the eggs?"

Nico laughs. "Can't give away my secret. But I think you're an easy audience with all the take out crap you eat."

After breakfast we share a shower. We stay in until we're both pruney and the water runs cold. I could have spent hours sudsing up all the hard lines on Nico. He's even more sexy in the full light of day. His broad square shoulders lead to his thick tattooed and rippled arms. His flat abdominal muscles feel as if they're carved of stone and he has the most delicious v that points down to his impressive manhood. Truly a work of art.

Nico tells me he wants to take me out for the day and I agree, although he won't tell me where we are going. We pass through the gym on the way out and I'm surprised at how packed it is for a Sunday. A lot of shouted greetings are exchanged and Nico waves and keeps us moving. I hear a catcall or two as we make our way to the garage and I feel Nico's grip tighten on my hip.

He opens the door to the SUV for me and helps me in. "Sorry about that. Sunday is match day and it's a testosterone fest. They come in pumped up to compete and their manners go out the window."

I smile. "It's fine. Doesn't bother me. I waitressed through college at a place that hosted private bachelor parties every weekend. I learned to smile and ignore real fast."

"Yeah, well, I'll be kicking some asses when I get back, all the same."

We pull up at Navy Pier Park and Nico comes around to open my door. He helps me out of the SUV, but doesn't release my hand. Together we walk with our fingers laced tightly from the parking garage toward the Ferris wheel. I've never been one for public displays of affection, but it feels good, oddly natural, not forced or contrite.

There's a fair going on, as there is most summer weekends down at the pier, and vendors are set up all over the park. We walk around for a little while and the way that Nico directs us, I feel like we have a destination to get to eventually. But I don't ask. It's so unlike me to go with the flow and let someone else take the lead.

We come upon a bunch of tables set up, covered in Girl Scout cookies and dozens of girls in scout uniforms. A little girl is charging in our direction and for a minute I think she is running away from someone. Her face is so intent on where she is going. I can't help but smile when I see her smile, her entire face lit up like a Christmas tree on Christmas morning as she yells, "Uncle Nico, you came!"

Nico lifts her up and swings her into the air as the little girl is about to crash into us. "Yeah squirt, I came. You asked me to, right?" He sets her back down on the ground and she grabs Nico's hand and begins pulling him in the direction of the cookie table. Nico looks to me apologetically, and grabs my hand, pulling me with him. We're a human train led by what looks to be a six or seven-year-old girl.

"This is my Uncle Nico and he's famous!" The little girl yells to her friends. A gang of little girls swarm Nico and it's the first time I see the big tough guy look a little scared.

A woman stands next to me and introduces herself as Katie, Sarah's mom. She apologizes for her daughter's excitement and tells me that Uncle Nico is very popular with his nieces and nephews. I'm listening to her talk, but I can't tear my eyes from Nico as he interacts with the kids. He's such a walking contradiction, everything that he doesn't appear to be. Soft, gentle, sweet, and playful, nothing like the bad boy fighter who I first laid eyes on more than a year ago at a random fight that I had no business being at.

As if he senses me watching him, Nico looks up at me and catches me watching him. He smiles at me and I smile back. When I finally tear my gaze from the man who has captured my attention like no other, I find Katie is staring at me smiling. "What?" For a second I think I must have missed something during my momentary lapse of consciousness.

"Oh boy. You're in trouble. I know that look he has. It's the look of determination and the Hunter boys don't stop till they get what they want."

I laugh off her comment, but the thought that I could be Nico Hunter's prey makes my stomach do a little flip flop.

CHAPTER 23

Nico

"We're all set. Five weeks from Saturday you take on Kravits. The Commissioner himself gave me his word that it's a one win hurdle to the title bout. You kick Kravits' ass and we're back in the belt." Preach always sets me up, knows what I want to take away from a fight.

I nod and start swinging the jump rope.

"They want some new pics for the promo by Wednesday. Their dime, their shoot. All we have to do is bring the girls you want in the shots with you for the eye candy."

I whip the rope faster, taking two turns with each jump. "No girls."

Preach looks at me like I have two heads. "Whatta you mean, no girls. You're Nico the fucking Lady Killer. Your shots always have ladies."

I can hear the rope slicing through the air, each turn whistling as I increase the speed. "Yeah, well. Not this time."

Preach squints as if he's trying to read words that are written across my forehead. "This have anything to do with the girl?"

I don't respond. It's none of his business anyway.

Preach ratcheted up the workout today and I'll probably be sore as hell tomorrow, but right now I'm running on sheer adrenaline. I do an extra five mile run after he leaves, sprinting almost the entire time. I just can't seem to tire myself out, I've felt this way for the last few days.

I let the hot water work its way into my muscles, blasting the shower on the massage setting. My muscles don't hurt yet, but I know they will when I come down. I'm restless and I can't seem to relax. I give in to the mental debate I've been having since yesterday about not coming on too strong with Elle. I don't want to scare her, but, fuck I want that woman. And more than in my bed. I send off a quick text, before I change my mind. I'm acting like such a pussy. *Can't get you out of my mind. What are you doing?* I'll throw the ball in her corner and see where things lead.

I'm surprised when my phone chimes back quickly, indicating a new text has arrived. *Me too. About to order dinner.*

What are you in the mood for? I deliver.

You.

I don't respond to the text, but twenty minutes later I'm at Elle's door.

She opens it and smiles. "Where's my dinner?"

"I'm right here."

CHAPTER 24

Elle

I barely shut the door when I find myself thrust up against it by six foot three inches of pure man. He's all strength and power and there is no mistaking he wants me. Badly. Almost as much as I want him at this very moment.

I can feel his thick erection as he pins me to the door with his hips. He's hard as steel and it makes me crazy to have so much clothing between us. I reach down for his zipper and yank it down in one desperate motion. The sound reverberates loudly between us and Nico growls as I reach in to free him. I need to touch him. Now. Feel his warm thick cock in my hands. Freeing him from his boxers, I give him one quick pump from the base to the tip, squeezing firmly as I slide my way up.

Nico tries to grab for my skirt, his actions as desperate as mine. But I catch him off guard and grab his hand to stop him. He stills. I know already he will stop to check that I'm okay, even in the throws of passion. I use the seconds that pass, as he gives me room to confirm I'm okay, to slide down the door that I'm cornered against and drop to my knees.

I look up at him under hooded eyes. "You said you were bringing me dinner."

The wide tip of his smooth cock glides past my lips and I'm rewarded with a groan and small burst of pre-ejaculation on my tongue. I suck hard on his thick head and pump my fist up and down the length of him. Another throaty groan makes my clit swell and I drown out everything but the desire to hear the sound again. I need to hear it. Need to know what I can do to him. That I can bring him to the same place he has brought me before. The place I haven't been able to stop thinking about for two full days.

I feel Nico's fingers thread into my hair, winding until his hands are tightly wrapped. I lick him from base to tip on the underside and then slowly repeat the action on the top. I can feel his eyes watching me. Even though I can't see his face, I know he is laser focused on me. As I reach the tip, I swirl my tongue around, giving him a good show, letting him watch as my tongue worships his thickness.

One last swirl and then I suck him in deeply, unexpectedly, taking him by surprise as I swallow him down my throat so far it's difficult to breathe. His already thick cock swells and I have to adjust my breathing to my nose in order to continue. A few short bobs and he glides in and out more easily. My throat muscles relax, opening for more of him to slide down my wet throat. Nico hisses out a deep breath and his hands in my hair tighten almost to the point of pain, but not quite. Then it happens. His body tenses and he begins to unravel, his hands wrapped in my hair pull tightly, and he corners my head against the door as he begins to slide in and out of my mouth, pushing his cock deeper into my throat. He growls as he fucks my mouth and the sound of him losing control has me on the brink of my own orgasm.

Nico's hands suddenly release my head on a loud throaty groan and I feel him begin to slide out of me. "I'm going to come, Babe." His voice is strained and I want to finish what I started. I need to finish. So I push forward as he begins to pull away and catch him back in my mouth just as he begins to spurt long streams of creamy hot semen. I swallow it down and greedily suck on his head, desperate to milk every last drop out of him.

After he is emptied, his body gone lax, Nico pulls me to my feet and lifts me, cradling me as he carries me into my apartment. He gently kisses my forehead as he walks to the couch, and sits with me still cradled tightly in his arms. "That was incredible." He kisses the top of my head and speaks gently. "Thank you."

I snuggle into his chest and look up at him. "I don't think it's proper etiquette to thank someone after oral sex." I'm coy in my response.

"I'm not much for etiquette, Babe. I say what I feel and I feel thankful. And not just about the blowjob."

A few hours later we lie in my bed, spent. Nico twists a lose strand of my hair around his finger as we talk. I've always been a sleep after sex person, preferring to avoid the lingering intimacy that comes after two people share their bodies. But it's different with Nico, I like the quiet time getting to know each other almost as much as the physical time. Both settle me, leave me feeling replete.

"I set a date for a fight."

Mindlessly, I trace the beautifully woven ink patterns on his thick chest, following the circular design lightly with my nail. "It's your first fight since..." My voice drops off, I don't know how to finish the sentence.

"Yeah." Nico's voice is low and contemplative, but it doesn't sound like I've upset him with my thoughtless question.

"How long's it been?"

"Too long." He pauses. "Since May 1st last year, a little over 13 months."

His answer tells me the day is etched in his mind. I bet he can recite the number of days and hours and seconds since it happened. It's always there, in the back of your mind, even when you aren't thinking about it. It never goes away. I should know.

"What made you decide it was time?"

A long moment passes as Nico contemplates his answer. "I don't really know...I'm just ready to move on." His arm pulls me closer and he kisses the top of my head. The gesture is so small, yet so big.

CHAPTER 25

Elle

"Good morning, Regina." I hand my friend a tall caramel latte as I walk in even later than my usual late.

"Looks like you had a good night." Regina raises one eyebrow with a knowing smirk.

I look down at myself, wondering if something is out of place. Is my shirt on backwards? How could she know? "Are you joking? Is it that obvious?"

"Well you don't usually speak in singsong." She winks at me as I walk around her desk and lean against her file cabinet.

"Nico came over last night." I sigh, thinking back to the sight of him in my kitchen making me breakfast this morning wearing nothing but sweats that hung low on his waist in a sinfully delicious place.

"I guessed that by the just-fucked smile on your face."

"I thought it was my singsongy voice that gave me away?"

"That, and the flowers that came fifteen minutes before you walked in."

My day goes by in a rush of calls and work I hadn't planned on doing. But Leonard is due back soon and I want to make his first few days back easy, so I neglect my own files and spend more time with his.

I call Nico in the afternoon and thank him for the flowers. I love that he sent me wildflowers instead of something more common like roses. They're beautiful and colorful and befitting of the sender.

Regina and I both stay late and we order in dinner at the office. It's almost nine and our dinners are cold before we finally sit down in the conference room to take our first bites.

"Does he know?" Regina's usually direct and sarcastic voice is gentle and apprehensive. She knows what bringing up the past can do to me, so she steadies for my response.

"No."

Regina looks at me concerned. "Don't you think he'll understand... with what happened to him?"

I do. I really do think he'll understand for some reason. But I'm just not ready to say the words out loud yet. "Don't start, Regina. It's new and I'm not avoiding it, it just hasn't come up."

"It will never come up, unless you bring it up. How many years did you spend with William and it never came up?"

I sigh heavily, I know she's right, but I'm not ready for Nico to look at me differently. He'll see someone different once he knows. Or worse, he'll look at me with pity. The way he looks at me makes my heart skip a beat, something I'm only just learning to enjoy. Too many years of my life went by with me flatlining, trying to evade all emotions. It's the first time I want to feel in a long time. Feel the highs and the lows and all that's in between.

"I'm just not ready yet."

Regina knows what I've been through, so she doesn't push. But I know this isn't the last that I'll hear about it from her.

CHAPTER 26

Nico

"The chick the other night had some rack, hey Lady Killer?" Frank Lawson is a complete asshole. Always has been. I didn't even notice he was in the gym the other night when Elle and I walked through.

"She's not some chick and keep your eyes off her when she's in here, or you'll be finding a new place to train." The whole room goes quiet. "After I kick your ass."

Frank throws his hands up in exaggerated surrender and I hear a few of the guys quietly laugh in the background.

"Hey Frank, Nico can use a sparring partner, whatta you say?" Preach chimes in. Gotta love Preach always looking out for me. He just gave me an excuse to knock that asshole on his ass and call it practice.

My stare is icy when Frank looks at me. He knows I'm pissed. But the whole place is still quiet and now he'll look like a pussy if he says no. "Umm...sure."

Preach winks at me as I turn to finish my warm up. On a bad day I can take Frank with one hand tied behind my back. Today I won't need either.

A few hours later, Preach and I lock up and I make us both a protein shake. I need to replenish the calories, Preach is working on a little gut.

"Put some extra peanut butter in mine."

I slap Preach in the gut. "You don't need any extra peanut butter, old man."

"You better hope you look as good as I do when you're my age." He sucks in his gut and throws back his shoulders as he speaks.

"I'll worry about it in seventy or eighty years when I'm almost your age." I answer back to Preach with sarcasm. This is who we are. We bust chops, fight, argue, and get pissed off at each other. But he's like a father to me, the old bastard.

"Yeah, well, with the quantity of food you inhale, I'm thinking you might not make it to my ripe old age. Your new lady cook good?"

I laugh. "Ah, that would be a no. I made her eggs the other morning and she thought it was magic that I made them taste so good. All I put in was salt and pepper."

"Well then, it's a good thing she looks like that if she can't cook." Preach goads me.

"Watch it old man, or I'll knock you on your ass, too." I hand him his shake, with a double scoop of peanut butter.

CHAPTER 27

Elle

Friday night Regina and I go out for drinks after work. Our regular place is packed for happy hour, but we eventually manage to get two seats at the bar. I have two glasses of wine, while Regina has at least twice that. Nico is meeting me at the bar at eight and taking me to dinner and I don't want to be too tipsy. Anything over two inside of two or three hours is too much for me.

My back is to the crowded bar, I'm surprised when I hear a familiar voice I don't expect to hear. William. It's not that I don't want to see him, but the place we're at just isn't on William's revolving list of regular restaurants. I'm pretty sure Zagat's never stepped foot inside here.

"Hey, Elle." William greets me in the same manner he normally would in a public place. He kisses me on the cheek and gives me a slight brush of his hand on my hip. "Hey Regina." He gives her a smile, but no kiss on the cheek.

William introduces the man he's with as one of the new associates at his firm. He's older for an associate, but nice looking, a little on the shorter side. I'm surprised at the lack of awkwardness in our conversation. Oddly, it feels like nothing has changed. After a few minutes, we slip into easy conversation about one of the cases we had been discussing over the last year and Regina and the new guy seem to have found something they both find hysterical.

I have no idea how long we talk for, but it's nice, and I begin to think maybe William and I really can be friends. Maybe it's what we always were. I lose track of time, and let myself enjoy the familiarity of my conversation.

William's back is to Nico as he approaches the bar, but I catch sight of him the minute he walks through the door. My body responds to him instantly, my pulse increasing and my breaths coming shorter and faster. My eyes follow his every step and our eyes lock the minute he spots me. The crowded room falls away as he walks to me and I shift in my seat feeling tingly all over at the intensity in his gaze. God the man makes me feel so alive.

He's a few steps away when his eyes finally leave mine and catches the face of the man I'm talking to. Something in his face changes, his eyes are darker, wilder, when his eyes come back to me only a second or two later. William notices my distraction and traces my line of sight, turning as Nico reaches us.

Effortlessly, William makes the change from friend to businessman and greets Nico in the way I've watched him schmooze a hundred clients before. Nico nods his head curtly and I hear him say, "William," but he doesn't turn to acknowledge him and his eyes never release mine. The awkwardness that was missing with William, suddenly hangs thick in the air. Nico's face gives nothing away, but I can feel the tension emanating from his body.

His eyes squint ever so slightly as he studies me, looking for an answer to some unasked question. I'm still as Nico extends his arm toward me, his big hand gently hooking around my neck and pulling me slightly toward him as his head comes down to meet mine. His mouth covers mine and he plants a quick, dry kiss on my lips. His head pulls back slightly and he nods and speaks before he releases me. "Babe."

The look in his eyes is something I'm not used to, but there's no mistaking it's there. Jealousy, possessiveness. He's just marked his territory with one small move. The hint of a smile I see threatening in the corner of his mouth tells me he knew exactly what he was doing. The independent woman inside of me tells me I should be pissed, finding his territorial action appalling, but my body refuses to listen. Instead, I'm aroused, finding his possessive gesture incredibly sexy and exciting.

Regina breaks me out of my daze with her words and I find the three people we are with staring at me. I forgot there was anyone else in the room. "Do I get a greeting like that too?" Her sarcastic comment seems to break the awkward silence, and Nico responds sweetly by giving her a kiss on the cheek and treating her to his sexy grin. "Hey, Regina." She giggles like a schoolgirl at his touch. My friend definitely has a new crush.

William looks confused, almost shell shocked for a minute. His reaction surprises me, not that he reacts, but that he allows me to see it on his face. I've watched him bluff in negotiations and cover his surprise to testimony on the witness stand, without ever a hint of reveal on the outside. He's a master at maintaining a poker face, but I think Nico's kiss must have caught him very off guard.

Nico extends his hand to me. "Ready?"

I smile hesitantly at William and say my goodbyes to everyone before putting my hand in Nico's and rising to leave.

The restaurant is in the back of the bar and it's quieter and more intimate. Nico pulls out my chair before sitting and the waitress takes our drink order as soon as we're both seated. We're finally alone and Nico is looking at me questioningly. He seems to be expecting me to say something, but I don't. I wait, I want to know what's on his mind.

"Drinks with William?" His voice is low and he sounds angry. I can tell he's doing his best to appear controlled.

"It wasn't a planned thing, if that's what you're asking." I raise an eyebrow in question. But I know exactly what he's asking.

Nico studies me for a second and then nods, accepting my answer.

Dinner is good, although I think Nico's cooking is better. We move past whatever issue he had with William and Nico has me laughing through most of dinner, telling me more stories about growing up with his three brothers. His childhood memories are beautiful, filled with laughter and fighting and a roller coaster of emotions that always seem to land on love. It's so different than the memories I've spent half my life trying to keep at bay.

The sprawling lawn that lead to our stately home looked beautiful, like something from a tender storybook. Yet inside was anything but, instead filled with anger and violence. It should have been easy for us. We were a family. Two parents and none of the financial stresses that many have to face daily. Yet Nico's single mom, who struggled raising four boys, seems to have been able to give them so much more. I'll never understand why we lived the way we did.

The waitress arrives with our check and she looks at Nico shyly. "Umm…can I bother you for your autograph? I'm a huge fan." She's nervously swaying back and forth as she speaks and it's sweet, almost coquettish. I hadn't really noticed her before. She's a pretty girl, something about her has a girl-next-door quality.

Nico smiles and tells her he's happy to sign an autograph and the two of them spend a few minutes talking about his upcoming fight. Her shyness easily disappears as they talk and I watch as he turns her from shy girl to flirty woman in just under three minutes. The transformation in her is remarkable. But it's Nico who brings it out of her. He gives her his full attention as she speaks, it's just shy of flirting and he doesn't even try. Whatever he has exudes from him naturally. By the time they're done, the sweetness that I felt when the doe-eyed waitress asked him for a simple autograph has turned into something else. I'm pretty sure that something else is jealousy, but it's new to me.

Nico turns to me, "You ready?" He stands and offers me his hand.

"Sure, if you're done." My response comes out more sarcastic than I intended, but I give him my hand nevertheless.

Nico's eyebrows arch in surprise at my tone and he looks at me at first in confusion, and then it quickly turns to amusement. He pulls me to him and crushes my mouth to his. He doesn't care that we're standing in the middle of a crowded restaurant, and he makes it so that I don't either.

We no longer invite each other in at the end of the night, it's just a given. I spent years dating William and we never moved past the invite stage to where Nico and I have gone in only a few weeks. I don't know when it changed, but I think we've left dating and moved into relationship. It just happened. Something slipped by me and it was too late before I noticed. Not that I would have stopped it anyway. But I find it intriguing when I look back to where things stayed with others. This man does something to me that's different. It's like breathing. I don't think about it, my body and brain just work together of their own accord to take care of my need for air. Nico's become a need.

We settle into my apartment and Nico sits in the loveseat facing the couch. It looks more like a big chair with his large frame filling up so much space. I kick off my heels and walk towards the couch.

"Come here." His voice is gruff and sends a chill up my spine. He extends his arm up and pulls me down to him so that I'm sitting facing him, straddling his muscular thighs. I squirm a bit to find a comfortable place, but I feel his thick bulge beneath me and there is no place to hide with my legs spread so widely over him. He looks amused watching me, so I settle on a spot even though he's pressed up against me in my most intimate of areas. I feel an ache almost immediately.

"You have a jealous streak in you." His eyes light up as he pushes my hair back off of my face with his calloused fingers. He leans in ever so slightly and kisses me gently on the lips before he speaks, his lips still so close to mine I can feel the vibration of his words. "I like it."

"And you, what was that little thing you did with William?" My words come out breathless from his sweet kiss, but his body tenses underneath me at the mention of William.

Nico pulls his face back to look at me and he grips my hips tightly. "I told you I'm not sharing you." His voice is serious and rough.

I don't know how to respond to that, so I'm honest. "William and I have been friends since law school. He's a good friend."

Nico looks at me, waiting for more.

"We sort of, you know, added to the friendship a few years back." I blush and bite my lower lip unconsciously.

Nico's jaw flexes and his green eyes go dark, cloudy gray. "And now?"

"Now we're friends again. I guess. I haven't seen him since I told him that I didn't want to see him anymore, in that way. Tonight was the first time I've seen him since you and I started seeing each other."

Nico nods. His face tells me he understands that he wasn't my first, but it's difficult for him to hear. Difficult to accept the thought of me with another man. I want him to forget about William, put all thoughts of our pasts out of his mind and focus on me. Us. Now.

I lean forward and press my body up against his, the slight shift lines the length of him up against me. I can't help but let out a small moan as I feel him hardening underneath me.

"You're mine now." He groans as I push my weight down on him, the outline of him pushing up against me firmly through our clothes.

"Does that mean I get to do whatever I want with you then?" I flirt in a suggestive tone and raise one eyebrow in question.

"Only if that means I'm buried inside of you within the next few minutes."

His words ratchet up my arousal and I can't get to his bare skin fast enough. I begin to unbutton his shirt, my fingers frantic to unwrap the prize underneath. I make it two buttons when Nico reaches behind him and grabs the back of his shirt and pulls it over his head in one muscular yank.

I take in the sight of his bare chest, all defined and bulging. The plentiful ink woven on his arms looks like art on the most beautiful canvas I've ever laid eyes on. Lucky ink. I trace the lines on his chest, the crevices separating one muscle from another, allowing my fingernail to scrape lightly against his beautiful tanned skin.

His chest heaves up and down as he watches me touch him. I circle a trail around his taut nipple and then slowly reach down and flick it with my tongue before I gently bite down. Nico groans and his grip on my hips tightens and his head falls back as he takes a deep breath, struggling to maintain his control.

His neck exposed, I lean in and kiss gently once at the base of his neck, then move up slightly and bite gently. I alternate between gentle kisses and nipping as I work my way up his neck. When I reach his ear, I stop and whisper, allowing the hot breath from my words to float as I speak. "I'm on the pill and I'm clean, if…"

Nico doesn't give me a chance to even finish my sentence. My shirt is up and off of my head before I even realize he's taken over. Raw need floods through me in reaction to the intensity of his movement, and my body shivers when he roughly pushes down the cup to my bra and takes my nipple into his mouth. I whimper when he bites down and sucks hard while his hands lift me to take off my skirt.

He takes my mouth hungrily and I rub myself up against him, my swollen clit desperate for friction. A throaty moan escapes when I feel how hard he is and begin to ride him up and down through what remains of our clothes. With one strong arm, Nico lifts my ass and his other hand unzips his pants, freeing himself. "I've wanted to come inside of you so badly it hurts. Feel that clenching little pussy slide up and down my bare cock. I need in. Now."

It's a testament to our desperation that we don't even remove my panties or take down Nico's pants. He just pushes them aside to make enough room for us to connect before he lifts me high and positions the tip of him at my opening. I think he's just about to pull me down, spearing himself into me and I can't wait. But then he stills…he's shaking. "Shit. I don't want to hurt you. You take me as slowly as you need."

I need him. I don't care if it hurts or if my body isn't ready to take him all in at once. I have to have him inside of me. Filling me. All of me. Now. I surprise him when I force the weight of me down and take him in fully in one long, agonizingly blissful stroke. Nico closes his eyes for a second and groans loudly. I'm flush against the base of him and give my body only a few seconds to adjust to accommodate the length of him.

Nico takes my earlobe in his teeth and bites down, sending a burst of pain-pleasure down to the tips of my toes. "Ride me. You're so tight and wet. I'm going to fill up that sexy little pussy and make it mine. I want my smell on you. In you. So that the whole god damn world knows you're mine."

I gasp at his dirty words. They excite me. Fuel me. I feel my orgasm on the brink and I haven't even moved yet. Then I begin to ride him. Fast. Hard. Wet. We're both soaked with a sheen of sweat and our bodies slip slide up and down each other as I lift up and slam down, over and over again. Nico gyrates his hips up to meet my downward motion with each thrust and we both explode together. I feel his body harden as he releases into me and he pushes deeper and harder with each hot burst. It's as if he wants to get all of him inside of me so deep it can never escape. I know how he feels, because I feel the exact same way.

Minutes later, my lifeless body sags on his lap but he's still inside of me. Still hard even after such a powerful orgasm. He pushes back my dampened hair and sweetly kisses my forehead, holding me tightly to his chest for a minute. He stands, cradling my limp body in his arm and carries me to the bedroom, gently placing me down on the bed. He takes off his pants and crawls into bed, his naked body spooned behind mine, his arms wrapped tightly around me. As I drift off to sleep, I hear him say two words quietly. "Thank you."

Neither of us has moved when I wake the next morning.

CHAPTER 28

Nico

"Must be nice to have a lawyer make house calls." Preach tilts his chin toward the front desk where Sal is pointing Elle in my direction. She smiles at me and I smile back on a draw down. I'm thirty pull ups out from finishing my morning workout, but seeing Elle gives me a burst of adrenaline and it suddenly doesn't feel like I've already chinned seventy.

It's been more than a month now, and I'm still as into her as the day I met her. She has no idea how sexy she is. Her body is hot as hell when she's naked underneath me, but she totally rocks the whole sexy librarian look when she's dressed in those little, fitted, skirt suits for work.

"Hey, Preach."

"Hiya, Elle. Your boy will be done in a few minutes."

She looks at me as I pull up on the bar and I watch her take in my shirtless torso as it flexes to bring my weight up and down. Fuck, the way she looks at me like she wants to eat me, kills me sometimes.

"I kinda like him up there. Maybe you can make him do some extra for me today?" She teases Preach and he laughs.

"You hear that Nico, the woman doesn't think you're working hard enough."

I finish my last pull up and jump from the bar. I sweated clear through two shirts this morning and I'm soaked again. Dripping, since I discarded the second shirt an hour ago.

Sporting a mischievous grin, I walk with purpose the few steps between Elle and me and lift her, rubbing my sweaty body all over her pretty crisp suit. "Is that so, you think I'm slacking, huh?" She screeches at me to put her down, but I hear the smile in her voice as she smacks my back in protest of my sweaty body ruining her suit.

I place her down gently on her feet and give her a kiss on the mouth. She pretends to be pissed, but she's not and we both know it. But we'll play anyway.

"I come all the way over here to pick up these contracts and this is the thanks I get." She motions to the wet marks I've left on her suit. "Next time you'll be sending a messenger over to deliver them to me."

Preach walks away laughing. "Come on, I'll take a quick shower upstairs and you can take a look at the part I don't understand. I'll let you watch me in the shower to make it up to you." I wink at her and take her hand and start toward the elevator without waiting for her response.

CHAPTER 29

Elle

Nico comes out of the shower in a towel and I'm already sitting at the table half way done with the contract he wants me to look at. He comes up behind me and moves my hair from one side of my neck before reaching down to nuzzle me. He rubs his nose along the side of my neck and breathes deep. "You smell so good."

"I used to."

He chuckles and comes around the table to sit on the other side, opposite of me.

"I'm not done reading yet, but what part don't you like. I don't see anything too unusual so far."

"That's because you haven't read my other ones." Nico leans his elbows on the table and clasps his hands together. It's a common every day posture, but there's nothing common about it when Nico Hunter does it. His normally muscular biceps are huge, even more defined from his morning workout. Everything about him is just so purely, deliciously male. His square jaw, his green eyes that turn grey with desire when he comes near me, the way he looks at me like he's a hunter and I'm his prey. He's incredibly distracting. Even more so sitting in nothing but a towel. Lucky towel.

I bring my eyes back to his and he's watching me with the sexy half grin that makes me melt and I know I've been caught looking at him.

"See something you like, Babe?" His voice is raspy and sexy as all hell.

"What? No! This is strictly a professional visit. I have to get back to the office. William is coming at three for a deposition on a case where we have co-defendants and I want to read this through before I pass it to him."

Nico's jaw flexes and his playfulness is gone. The mention of spending my afternoon with William has the effect of throwing a bucket of cold water on him.

"Glad I coated you with my sweat now. It'll keep the other lions away."

I roll my eyes at him. He half pretends he's kidding, but I know he's probably really happy with himself that I'll be spending the afternoon with William while wearing his scent.

"Back to business." I point down at the contract. "Why don't you tell me what I'm looking for so it's easy to find then?"

"Well, there's three things that don't sit right with me." He counts them off on his fingers for me. "It's three times the amount of money that I got last time for a title fight. They added a dropout clause for Preach. And they don't have to name the contender until seven days before the fight."

"Okay, let's take them one at a time. Three times the amount of money. Doesn't sound like a bad thing to me. What has you concerned there?"

"Nothing really. I like that part. But it's not really necessary. So it makes me wonder why they're throwing it at me. I know a rematch for my title is a moneymaker, but we would have expected one and a half times what I took for the first title fight."

"Okay, is adding a dropout clause for Preach unusual?"

"Yeah. He's never had one before. If I dropout after they sell the fight, I pay a hefty penalty. It makes sense. They spent it and they want me to make them whole. It's a common clause for a fighter. But why Preach? As far as I know, they never put the trainer or manager on the

120

hook too. And his is almost as big as mine. Mine is risk vs. reward. But his is all risk."

"Hmm. What possible reason could they have for wanting to put Preach on the hook?"

"At first I thought they could be planning on spending a lot of cash before the fight and they were looking to lessen the blow by splitting it between us. But I told them I'd take Preach's dropout penalty on my contract and they said no. They won't let me take on his risk."

"So that means it's not about money, they want Preach invested. What reason could they have for wanting your trainer invested? Other than they want you to win badly and they think he will work you harder."

"I don't know. But it just doesn't feel right to me. Preach is fine with it. He knows I'm in for the haul and won't screw him. But it still bothers me."

"Interesting. Let me give it some thought…maybe I can think of a different angle since I'm an outsider. What about the unnamed fighter?"

"Usually you know who you're gonna fight before the fight. I guess mine is a little different because I never technically lost my title and the guy who holds it now just retired because of an eye injury. So there's no clear opponent, although we all assume it will be Caputo, he's the next highest ranked guy."

"Do you study your opponents?"

"Of course."

"So everyone who is a possible contender spends months studying you, but you could be studying the wrong guy and only find out seven days before?"

Nico leans back in his chair. "Yep."

"Which term bothers you the most?"

"Preach having a penalty clause."

"Not the part about not knowing who you're going to fight?"

"Nah." He crosses his arms over his bare chest. "I don't need more than a day or two to learn a fighter's moves."

"Okay. How long do we have?"

"Two days."

"What's the rush? I thought you had at least two months after the fight this weekend before your next fight?"

"I do. But they want this signed before my qualifying fight this weekend. The deal isn't a go unless I win, but they want it wrapped up before the weekend anyway."

"Okay. Let me work on it." I stand. "I should get going. I need to give my file a quick read before my afternoon deposition."

Nico stands and grips me tightly against his body when I attempt to leave after a nice goodbye kiss.

"Twenty minutes."

"I'll be late."

"I'll be good."

"I'm sure you would. But..."

My objection goes unheard when Nico's mouth crashes down on mine. He kisses me long and hard with his naked muscles pressed up against me until my body defies my brain and succumbs to his demand.

An hour later I'm on my way back to the office, with Nico's scent on my clothes and inside of me. I have a sneaking suspicion that Nico wanted it that way, knowing I was seeing William.

CHAPTER 30

Elle

I haven't seen or heard from William since the night at the bar when Nico decided to out us as a couple by kissing me purposefully right in front of him. Now I'm going to sit next to him in an all afternoon deposition with Nico's scent on me and my underwear still damp from our mid day romp. I should really be pissed off at Nico for being such a neanderthal, but I can't help but smile when I think about him wanting to mark me as his. It's archaic and adolescent and the man is turning me into a foe for the women's liberation movement, but god damn it, the man may well be my kryptonite.

Our co-clients are here early, earlier than William, which is unusual. He is normally the first one to arrive for everything. I put our clients in one conference room and the opposition in another room and go back to my office to review my notes. Regina buzzes me from the desk to let me know that William has arrived and I go out to the lobby to greet him with a little trepidation.

Unlike last time, and every other time we've seen each other over the last few years, he doesn't kiss me hello, not even a kiss on the cheek. He's professional, but distant. Immediately I can tell that he doesn't want to talk about anything but business. Even my attempt at cordial small talk when I greet him is met with resistance.

"How are you?" I ask, in an attempt to put a feeler out for how things are going to be between us.

"Fine. Are our clients here?" He's not even going to reciprocate my polite banter to inquire how I am.

"Yes, they're in the conference room. Do we need to put together a game plan before we start?" We work well together and it's usually not necessary, but we always spend a few minutes talking before we meet with our clients. Go over strategy or pitfalls we want to review.

"No. Unless you're not ready."

So that's how it's going to be? I straighten my spine and stand tall. I can do impersonal with the best of them. "I'm ready."

An hour into our deposition, the ice between William and I thaws. Twice, we both went to ask the same question at the same time. Then we both grabbed for the water pitcher at the center of the table at the same moment. Even opposing counsel got a kick out of how we can finish each other's sentences. We really are good together. Or were, I should be thinking were.

We are almost ready to wrap up for the day and I watch William as he finishes up the last of his questions. He's intelligent and well-spoken and undeniably handsome. Financially sound, stable, and dependable. I don't know what was missing. William catches my stare as he turns to me to ask if I have any other questions to ask, and I become a little flustered at being caught admiring him.

We make our way to the reception area to see our clients out and Regina tells me she's going to head out on time for a change. She has a hair appointment. I smile and lie when I tell her that I'm not that far behind her. Both of us know I'll be here for hours more. William walks back to the conference room with me and we spend a few minutes talking about the case. There really weren't any surprises, but I'm glad we have the chance to talk before he goes. He's friendly and less guarded and we easily slip back into our usual banter for a while.

I excuse myself and head to the ladies' room. When I get back to the conference room, William is almost done packing up both our files. I'd have to unpack it and reorganize my files if it was anyone else, but I'm sure that William packed it away just as I would have. We're a lot alike, both methodical in our work habits. I still have to speak to him about Nico's contract, but it feels almost awkward to bring him up.

"Umm. I have a fight contract for you to look at."

William stops packing the case and looks up at me. He seems confused for a second and then recognizes what I'm referring to and nods.

I walk next door to my office to get the envelope where I've stashed it with some of the notes I jotted down while I was with Nico. I'm surprised when I look up and William is standing in the doorway of my office. I walk to him and hand him the envelope. He doesn't move from the doorway.

"Is he why we stopped spending time together?" William's voice is quiet when he speaks.

I'm not sure how to answer the question. The truth is, it is the reason why I stopped seeing William, but not for the reason he thinks, but it seems rude to say it for some reason.

I look up at him and without realizing it, I bite my lip.

William looks at me and nods as if he understands, but then reaches his hand out and tugs at my lip where I'm biting. He keeps his finger on my lip after I release it from between my teeth and he rubs at the spot where I've probably left an indent.

"That always did drive me crazy." He says with a small smile and a low voice, his eyes still focused on my lips as he speaks.

"What?" I sound confused, because I am. I have no idea what he means.

"You bite your lip when you're nervous. It's your tell." William smiles and glances quickly between my mouth and eyes before he continues. "Since you're superwoman, I didn't see it very often, but I always thought it was sexy when it came out."

William is still standing in my doorframe and now, between his words and his lingering touch on my mouth, the moment feels intimate. I don't know what to say, so instead I stand there like an idiot. He's caught me off guard, he's always been an easy read. His finger that traced my lip falls away, but his hand moves to my neck. It all happens in slow motion and yet I don't have time to stop it as he lowers his face to mine and kisses me on the mouth.

I'm shocked. Not at the kiss itself, but because I never would have expected it from William. It takes me a second or two before I snap out of it and realize I haven't pulled away. But then I do. I pull my head back and look up at William, who I expect to be offended, or pissed, or just something…anything, other than what I find. He's smiling. Like a Cheshire cat, a big ole grin on his face and I have no idea what to make of it.

I'm still standing perfectly still with Nico's envelope in my hand, when William takes the envelope and leans down to whisper in my ear. "We're good together, I'll be here if you change your mind."

After a long day, I usually have a glass of wine to help unwind and relax. Sometimes I take a bath to help my tense muscles loosen. Tonight I'm on my second glass *and* I'm running a bath. Between Nico in the morning and William in the afternoon, I'm in need of a little liquid assistance to unfrazzle my brain.

I sit in the warm water and soak, my head barely sticking up out of the water. It's so warm and soothing and eventually, after a few minutes, I feel what amounts to a sigh roll through my body as it gives in to my deep breaths in my pursuit of calm. There's serenity in the stillness of the water and my body absorbs it through my pours, desperate to find its peace.

When I'm sufficiently relaxed, I finally allow my brain to rehash my day. I replay William's kiss in my head. It was sweet. Nice. Familiar.

And oddly bold for William. But it was his smile and words afterward that were most surprising. He thinks Nico won't work. That eventually I'll come back to my senses and things will be back to normal. I should probably be annoyed with his assumption. But, honestly, how could I blame him? Even I thought Nico was wrong for me. I spent years convincing myself what I wanted, what's good for me. I've done such a good job that William believes he knows better too.

I dismiss the thoughts of William quickly and spend the rest of my heavenly soak thinking about only one man. Nico Hunter. The way he touches me. Grips me so tight, like he has to, like there's no other choice. I think back to his hands on me today. He doesn't just run his hands down my body feeling my curves, his finger tips press into me as he feels me. Really feels me. In a way that I know he's enjoying touching me almost as much as I'm enjoying being touched. Before Nico, I didn't even know there was a difference in the way a man could rub his hand down my side. But there is, and the difference is mind-shattering. I'm a few seconds away from pleasuring myself to a vision of Nico in my head when my phone, sitting on the sink, rings and breaks me out of my fantasy. It startles me, and I end up splashing water all over the floor when I jump.

I do a poor job of drying off my hands and settle back into the tub as I answer. Speak of the devil. "Hey." His voice is gravelly and low and the sound of it sends a shiver through my body even though I'm soaking in a warm bath. I feel like a teenager again. Excited to hear a boy's voice on the other end of the phone.

"Hey. How was your day?"

"The middle part was great."

I smile, even though he can't see me. Yep, I'm a school girl with a crush so big, I'm smiling when he says hello on the phone.

"Mmmm…that was my favorite part of the day too."

Nico chuckles. "Where are you? You sound like you're in a tunnel or something."

"In the bathtub."

Nico lets out a loud rush of air and his voice turns low and gruff. "You're naked right now?"

"Yep. And I was just thinking about you when the phone rang."

"Oh yeah, what were you thinking about?"

"The way you touch me."

Nico groans. "Were you touching yourself?"

My answer is honest and comes out before I can think better of offering the truth. "I think I might have if you hadn't called."

"Shit." Then he's quiet for a long minute and I wait for him to say more, but he doesn't.

"What's the matter?"

"You're killing me, Elle. I feel like I'm fourteen with you. I'm walking around with a hard-on half the time from just thinking about you. I'm never going to be able to sleep tonight now."

I smile, feeling satisfied somehow that I'm not the only one who feels like a hormonally crazed teen. "Maybe you should try a bath."

Nico is quiet for a minute. I'm just about to ask if he's still there when he finally speaks. His voice is low, "Touch yourself for me, Babe." The words are strained and thick, they hang in the air surrounding me.

"I...I've never..." I want to tell him that I've never had phone sex or masturbated for a man before, but the words are stuck in my throat.

"You can." Nico senses my hesitation and isn't going to allow it.

"It's not..."

"Are your nipples hard?" God I even love his voice.

I look down at my nipples, they're barely covered by the water. They're swollen and protruding and I think they have become even more engorged in just the last few minutes.

"Yes." My answer comes out a whisper.

"Feel one. Rub your finger over the top of it for me."

I push aside my hesitation and do what he asks. Slowly, I graze my finger over my hard nipple making a small circle. My already swollen nipples respond, and swell even more, enough so they are no longer

128

below the surface of the water. Now the full tips are sticking out from the still water of the bath. No longer protected by the warm soak, the cool air meets the swells and it's as if every nerve in my body is connected to the small protruding nubs peeking out. A jolt of electricity travels through my entire body. If I had closed my eyes, I would have sworn that Nico just blew on them. The sensation surprises me and I don't even try to mask the gasp that comes out.

Nico groans. "Pinch it. Hard."

I do. I grasp my swollen nipple between my fingers and firmly squeeze. Another wave of electricity travels through my nerve endings. Only this time all of the different paths traveled arrive at the same place, at the exact same moment...my clit. The swell of my nipples is now seemingly connected to the swell between my legs. A low moan escapes my lips.

"It feels good doesn't it, Babe?"

"Yes." I admit, my hesitation slowly melting away.

"You need to put your phone on speakerphone. Put it down close to you."

I do as he asks.

"Close your eyes."

Nico's voice on the speaker of my phone makes what we're doing feel even more intimate, as if he could really be standing near me telling me what to do. I close my eyes, ready to imagine he's in the room with me.

"Take your other hand and touch your clit. I know it's swollen for me already. Pretend I'm there with you, watching you. I'm sitting behind you, looking at you touch yourself. It makes me hard to watch you. You're so damn sexy."

I slip my hand down my body and let Nico's deep, familiar voice fill my senses. I can almost forget it's my own hand rubbing my aroused clit in small circles when I hear the need in his voice. It's so carnal. Another small groan escapes and Nico responds with a growl, a sound echoing pure male pleasure. It makes me bold.

"Are you hard?" I finally find the courage down deep to do more than listen.

"Hard like stone. I want inside of you so bad. Deep inside of you. I need to fill up that tight little pussy, baby."

Oh god. My body clenches at his words and I feel them, literally feel his words roll through my body.

"Is that what you want? You want my hard cock inside of you, don't you?"

"Yes." My voice is raspy and needy. I push myself back harder against the wall of the tub, my ass rubbing up against the cast iron. I pretend it's Nico behind me. His hardness behind me as I sit between his legs and he watches me. Watches me touch myself.

"Take two fingers and slip them into that wet pussy. I need to be inside of you."

I hesitate for only a second before I do as he commands, plunging two fingers inside of myself deeply. There's an ache inside of me that I need to reach, but it's just out of grasp. A sound escapes my throat that is a cross between a moan and a word and I'm not even sure what the word was supposed to be.

"That's it, Babe. In and out. I'm inside of you. Harder." Nico's strained voice sounds as desperate for release as I feel. I picture him. His wide shoulders and straining muscular arms. His beautiful green eyes on me. Watching me. His hips thrusting down toward me. His long, thick cock. God, his cock.

"Oh God." I moan as I feel the unmistakable pulse pound through me as my orgasm begins to take hold.

"Come for me." Nico's firm, commanding tone detonates my climax and it spreads over me. I feel the spasm surround my fingers as my body begins to pulsate uncontrollably.

I hear Nico's name being called over and over, but it doesn't register that the sound is coming from me. It takes over me. I've completely surrendered to my orgasm and I pump my fingers in and out of myself as I ride my release until I'm chasing the last wave with small tremors in the aftershock.

A few minutes later both our voices sound different. They're hazy and loose and I wonder if we both may sleep better tonight. "Did you…" My voice trails off. I want to know if he finished. I'm not completely sure what I would do if he didn't, but now that I've found my bliss, I suddenly realize I have no idea if he was touching himself.

Nico chuckles at my non-question. "Yeah, Babe. We're both going to sleep good tonight."

CHAPTER 31

Elle

I find our seats at the fight and my stepbrother Max is excited at how close we're sitting. Ringside. Or, would it be cageside since technically there is no ring, but instead they fight in a cage? We weren't sitting this close at the first and only fight I'd been to, yet I still cringed with each blow. Violence is something I have steadfastly avoided since I was old enough to control my own path. Yet here I sit, about to watch someone I care about pummel another human being. Or worse, be pummeled himself. I barely slept a wink last night, fretting over coming here. Yet, I feel like my body is wide awake, oddly on high alert.

Lily, Nico's sister-in-law, arrives with her entourage and there is no doubt that the man standing next to her is Nico's older brother Joe. They're the spitting image of each other, only his brother is slightly shorter and carries a bit of a belly. Whereas Nico doesn't have an ounce of fat on his body. Lily introduces me to her husband and he smiles. It's Nico's smile, sans the dimples. Seeing it on another man's face is almost odd, but somehow it makes me warm to the man quickly. There's a sense of familiarity that puts me at ease because of the likeness.

Lily also introduces me to a teen named Vinny. I've heard Nico talk about him before. Actually, quite a bit. Nico's family have all unofficially adopted him, taking a strong interest in the boy with the bad home life. They seem to rally around him as a family, each providing different support where they can.

Vinny is wearing a shirt with a picture of Nico on it and he notices me checking it out.

"I took the picture." He holds up a camera proudly when he speaks.

"Well, it's a very cool shirt."

"You really like it?"

"I do." I smile at him. I can see Vinny has the same teen struggle going on that I often see in Max. He wants to be laid back and cool, but sometimes he has trouble hiding his excitement. It's adorable.

I think he assesses my sincerity. Then he nods his head once and continues. "I'll make you one. Nico will be all over his chick wearing a picture of him."

We all laugh at Vinny's comment, but I can't help but think the boy is right. Nico would so love me wearing a picture of him across my chest to ward off the other lions when he's not around. He's a smart kid, knows Nico well.

Vinny and my stepbrother become instant friends and I'm glad that it gives me some time to get to know Lily better before the fight starts. Plus, the boys will have more fun without me sitting between them and cringing at every blow.

I don't even realize that I'm fidgeting in my seat, but Lily does. "You nervous?" She smiles at me. It's a genuine smile and I get the feeling she finds my inability to sit still amusing for some reason.

"Is it that obvious?"

"Well, I figured it was either that or you have to go to the bathroom pretty bad with the way that leg's shaking." She motions with her head pointing to my leg, which is frantically tapping up and down. I hadn't even realized I was doing it. I smile at her and will my leg to steady.

"Fighting has never been my thing." It's the understatement of the year.

"Well, don't worry then." She pauses and sits up taller in her chair, a silent declaration of the confidence in her next words. "This isn't going to last more than thirty seconds. Nico can take this clown with one arm tied behind his back."

It's almost a full hour later before the opponents are called into the cage. I've sat through girls in skimpy bikinis holding up advertising signs, commentators giving their predictions on the fight, and Max and Vinny have each downed three hot dogs. Lily and Joe try to get me to have a beer with them. I know they're trying to help, get me to relax a little. But I'm aware of the effect alcohol has on my emotional state and I'm way too afraid to lose any control. I'm about to watch the man I'm crazy about do things that I'm nervous will dredge up bad memories. Memories I can't allow myself to associate with Nico Hunter.

"Ladies and Gentlemen, in the red corner, standing six-foot-three-inches tall, weighing in at two hundred and twenty-one pounds, he is the former heavyweight champion, he needs no introduction to the ladies…I give you Nico 'The Laaaaaaaadddyy Killllllllllllllllllller' Hunter." The crowd goes crazy, but not half as crazy as Vinny, who is jumping up and down and screaming so loud I can see the veins popping from the sides of his neck. Lily looks at me, then at Vinny, and then back to me and we both laugh, but no one can hear us standing next to Nico's number one fan.

Nico's opponent is introduced and he receives only a fraction of the cheers, plus some actually boo for the poor guy. Mostly Vinny and my stepbrother. The announcer goes through a bunch of rules and rattles off some information about disciplines, none of which means much to me. I make a mental note to learn more about the sport and file it away for my next afternoon alone with Google.

The two men turn to make their way to their respective corners and Nico is facing the crowd for the first time since he entered the arena. He is undeniably a feast for the eyes, every woman's fantasy. He's tall and gorgeous with a square jaw and eyes the color of jade. And his body, oh his body. I could get lost in the valleys that define his muscles. But I'm not the only one to notice. Women yell and catcall to him like construction workers when a miniskirt passes by in the heat of summer. Nico either doesn't care or he's so focused he won't let outside interference in. I figure he's probably an expert at drowning out the crowd. But then he turns his head and his eyes find mine instantly through the crowd. And hold. There's probably ten thousand screaming people in the room, but for a few quick seconds, there's only me and Nico. He doesn't smile or acknowledge me outwardly, but he wants to know I'm here. Watching him. Supporting him. And I finally realize, even with my past, there's no place I'd rather be.

The first round is only five minutes long, but it feels more like five hours. I quickly learn it's a lot more difficult to watch a fight when it's someone you care about inside the cage. The gates to the cage close and I take a deep breath, hoping Lily is right and I can exhale in thirty seconds when it's over.

Nico is holding his own, but it's definitely not the lopsided fight everyone seems to have expected. The break between rounds is short, but Preach seems to spend the entire time yelling at Nico. Something is off. I can see it in the way Preach yells and Nico tunes him out. It shows on Nico's brother's face too.

The two men are back at it after a rest that was too short for me to catch my breath, no less a fighter. There's less jumping around scathing at each other this time. The blows have started now and I watch as Nico's opponent lands a strike connecting directly to the left side of his jaw. A real wave of nausea rolls over me and for a second I think I might be physically sick. Nico looks pissed, but takes the hit in stride, without as much as a waiver of his balance. He hits him back and his opponent takes two steps back from the force of the strike, but he remains on his feet. Fall, god damn it, fall.

Eventually Nico forces his opponent to the ground and he's quickly put on his back with Nico on top of him. His opponent is completely exposed and it looks like Nico has the perfect opportunity to strike. I brace for what it looks like is about to come next to the poor man sprawled out on his back in such a vulnerable position. But then it never comes. A few seconds later his opponent is righting himself again and the two men take to a ground wrestle.

When the round finally ends, I peel my eyes away from the cage long enough to look at Lily. I feel desperate. "Is everything okay? It doesn't look like the easy fight you thought it would be?"

Lily looks at me and I see a flash of pain in her eyes. She's upset about the fight, but something in her expression tells me the pain has nothing to do with Nico's opponent being able to stand longer than everyone predicted. Lily opens her mouth to respond, but then stops and closes it. But Joe chimes in.

"He's afraid to hurt him. That's not Nico fighting up there. I've seen him strike harder sparring in his gym as a warm up."

Faster than I can take the enormity of the words that are slowly sinking in, the break is over and the two men meet back in the middle, ready for the final round. It's only a few seconds into the clock when his opponent strikes hard, hitting Nico with a kick to the ribs that looks like it could leave a few broken in its wake. Again, Nico doesn't flounder, he stands his ground. But something else happens, I see it in his face. He's pissed. Really pissed.

His response is to lunge at his opponent, taking him to the mat in one powerful takedown. Nico moves fast, and within seconds he has him in some convoluted hold that looks like if the guy moves a fraction of an inch, his arm will snap in two. Nico twists his body once to add pressure and the guy taps his hand against the mat, conceding the fight.

The crowd roars, some of the women are standing on their seats and waving banners telling Nico they love him. I'm elated that it's over, but somehow I can't find it inside of me to cheer. I know I should celebrate, he's won, but it doesn't feel like victory. After taking in the crowd, I turn to see Lily and Joe aren't celebrating either.

The announcer holds up Nico's hand, declaring him the winner, and I catch my first glimpse of him. He's not smiling either. His face is blank, devoid of any emotion and it sends a shiver down my spine. I notice he doesn't look my way, not even on his way out when he passes right by our row. It's the first time the shiver I get from Nico Hunter isn't welcomed.

CHAPTER 31

Elle

Max is excited to go back to see Nico after the fight. He's invited Vinny and the two of them are reenacting the fight, throwing air punches at each other as we make our way to the hall of the arena. There are more fights going on after Nico's, but I don't want to stay to watch them and the boys are anxious to see their role model anyway.

We show our backstage pass to the security guard, who looks like he should be in the cage instead of checking IDs. The boys are brimming with pride that we have backstage access and they wear their tags around their necks proudly. We follow the directions the security guard gave us down a flight of stairs and a series of long hallways. We're underneath the building and there is a bevy of fighters, trainers, and advertising people milling around. There's also more than a few groupie-looking-type women, each has less clothes on than the next. Vinny seems to recognize all the fighters and recites their statistics as they pass. The kid is a walking encyclopedia on the who's who in MMA fighting.

Eventually Room 153 comes into sight, where we were told Nico would be. The door is ajar and there's loud voices coming from its direction. As we get closer, I recognize the loud voice is Preach and he's not just speaking loudly, he's screaming like a madman.

"I thought we were past this shit! You told me you were ready.

You're not fucking ready. I got your body ready, but only you know what's in that thick skull of yours…"

I'm stopped outside the door listening, basically eavesdropping when I remember the boys are hearing it all too. "You two." I rummage in my purse and pull out a twenty-dollar bill. "Go back up and buy some pretzels and watch the next fight. Come back when it's over." Max starts to respond and complain and I hit him with the big sister death stare and point a finger back in the direction we just came from. "Now."

Vinny nudges my stepbrother, "Come on man," and the two begrudgingly turn to leave. Vinny's a smart kid, he quickly knows which battles to fight and which he will never win. He'll do okay in life.

Now that I've sent the boys away, I'm not sure what to do. Preach is still yelling and I haven't heard Nico say one word yet. Part of me feels like I shouldn't interrupt, but another part of me has the urge to go in and protect Nico. I knew something was off, but he won damn it, he doesn't deserve to be treated like this. The lioness in me wins out and I knock on the door once and then enter the room without waiting for a response.

Nico is sitting on a bench with his head in his hands looking down. His posture reminds me of a child that's getting scolded. It's defeated and disappointed. He doesn't look up when I enter, but Preach quiets momentarily and turns to me.

"Maybe you can talk some sense into his thick skull." Preach throws the towel he was holding on the floor and stalks out of the room, slamming the door as the exclamation point to end his final departing rant.

I wait a few seconds, long seconds where I actually hear the clock on the wall ticking behind me, but Nico still doesn't acknowledge me. He hasn't moved. So I take a deep breath and walk to him, stopping in front of the bench where he sits. I slowly reach down and put my hands on his shoulders. I'm unsure of what to say, but I want to comfort him somehow.

Gently, I glide my fingers back and forth over his warm skin in what I hope is a soothing motion. His shoulders untense slightly at my touch. "Are you okay?" My words are barely above a whisper.

Nico shakes his head. No.

"Are you physically hurt? Can I get you anything?"

Again, only a headshake no in response.

"Do you want to talk about it?"

Yet another shake of the head.

I stand there for a few more minutes, quietly, my hands on his shoulders and him with his head still bowed. It's the longest I've been near him without him touching me. He's right in front of me, but he's light years away. I want to help him so badly, need to make him feel better. But he still hasn't looked at me or spoken. I kneel down in front of him and fold my hands around his clasped ones and look up at his face. I'm so close, he can't avoid me anymore. He tilts his head up slightly and his eyes lift to mine. What I find looking back at me breaks my heart into a million little pieces. My normally strong, confident man's eyes are filled with unshed tears and he looks…broken. Scared. Sad. His face is filled with anguish as he looks at me. He still doesn't speak, but his eyes say it all.

I hear voices from the door and then there's a knock before Vinny and Max enter the room. I turn away for a split second to look at the boys and when I turn back to Nico the emotion on his face is gone. Replaced by a stony façade that I've never seen before.

"Get the boys out of here." A stern voice I don't expect to hear commands, taking me by surprise. It's cold and distant and it startles me to hear such a tone in Nico's voice. So much so that I look up at his face with my brow furrowed, confused, as if the words he just spoke were foreign. But if his intentions weren't clear the first time he speaks, there's no mistaking them the second. "Go home, Elle."

It takes me hours to fall asleep and when I finally do, I toss and turn all night restlessly. I can't get the look on Nico's face, when I kneeled before him, out of my head. It's one I'm all too familiar with. Sorrow. Shame. Self-loathing. That moment comes back to haunt you when you least expect it. Just when you think you've finally found a way to bury it somewhere deep inside yourself, it rears its ugly head and then you're back to square one. Back to relive the pain. The regret. The guilt. And the healing has to start all over again.

CHAPTER 33

Nico

I don't even notice my knuckles bleeding until Preach's loud voice pulls my attention from the bag. It's five a.m. and I've been at it for hours already. No matter how hard I go at it, I can't wear myself out enough to close my eyes and not see his face. The face that will haunt me for the rest of my remaining days.

"You been at it all night?" It's the first time Preach has spoken to me since the fight. He's yelled and ripped into me, but nothing he's said has required a response until now.

"Some."

"You're getting blood all over the bag. Go ice 'em." He doesn't give a shit about the bag, it's Preach's way to tell me to ease up.

I look down at my hands and see the mess I've made for the first time, even though they were always in my line of sight. There's cuts and blood covering my knuckles and most of my fingers. A few are swollen to twice their size and I'm pretty sure they're broken. But I don't feel any pain. I want to, but I'm numb.

I head to the gym's small kitchen in the corner and wrap my knuckles in ice. I don't bother cleaning the blood off my stained hands. Preach follows and offers me a bottle of water and three pills.

"Take em."

I know what they are without asking. A heavy duty sleeping pill and two pain killers. My cocktail of choice for almost three months after my last fight. Preach threw them all out one night, at least I thought he did, when I got myself to the point of self pity that I could no longer function without a handful. I was popping them like a kid with a bag full of M&Ms. When he took them away, it cost me almost ten grand. Ten grand worth of repairs when I ripped my own gym apart in anger because the damn doctor wouldn't write me a new script to replace what Preach took. I'm surprised he's even offering them to me now.

Preach pushes his hand cupping the pills further in my direction. "God damn it Nico, take the fucking things. You need to sleep, your body needs to rest and that stupid ass head of yours isn't going to shut down long enough to let it. You take em like they're supposed to be taken, a day or two to heal, not like fucking candy."

Hostilely, I take the pills and swallow them in one gulp and leave Preach standing there with the unopened water bottle in his hand.

Some of the regulars are starting to trickle in now and they yell their congratulations in my direction. I don't want to hear them, don't deserve anyone's well wishes.

CHAPTER 34

Elle

After not hearing from Nico last night after the fight or all day today, I head to his gym after work. He hasn't responded to my texts and my calls go straight to voicemail. Either he's ignoring me or his phone is off. All I need is to make sure he's okay. Worry has built inside of me all day and I find myself at almost a jog going from my car to the entrance of the gym.

The usual desk guy recognizes me and I ask if Nico is around. My worry ratchets up a notch when he tells me he hasn't seen him all day. Now I'm starting to wonder if he's lying unconscious somewhere with an undiagnosed head injury from the fight.

Preach spots me and calls my attention in his direction with a loud whistle and a shake of the head. He's holding the heavy bag while some guy with no neck is punching and kicking so fast, it looks like he's having a seizure.

I make my way over to Preach and the guy without the neck stops hitting the bag and gives me a leering smile. It's a smile and look that makes me want to shower. Immediately.

"That's Nico's girl you big moron. He catches you looking at her like that, you're gonna be looking for a new gym. *After* you spend ten minutes looking for your teeth." Preach's tone isn't playful when he speaks.

I give a half-hearted smile to Preach. "Have you seen Nico? He hasn't answered my calls all day."

"I put him to bed this morning." Preach looks at me and then back to neckless. "Make yourself invisible for ten minutes."

Without complaint, neckless disappears. If I wasn't out of sorts, I'd probably find it oddly amusing, the power that Preach has over men twice his size. "You had to put him to bed? Is he okay?"

Preach pulls a towel from his back pocket and wipes his hands as he speaks. "He's got some issues, Elle, you know this already, right?"

"You mean what kept him from going back in the cage?"

"Yeah, that. Well, I found him trying to exhaust his body into submission to get some sleep. It's how he deals with things. He trains. Hard. Too hard sometimes. I think he'd been at it all night. Screwed up his hands. They'll heal. But other than that, I think the worst of it's in his head. I can fix the body. I can't fix what's in here." Preach's pointer finger taps on the side of his head.

"So how did you get him to go to sleep?"

"Drugs." Preach states matter-of-factly and without remorse.

"You gave him drugs?"

"Don't look at me like I'm the devil. They're his drugs. Doc prescribed 'em for him after the last fight. He started taking them too much so I took 'em away. But he needed 'em this morning, so I gave him enough to get him some sleep. The boy's got more energy than anyone I've ever met when he's on a tear. But the longer the tear, the harder the recovery. Nipped this one in the bud."

"Has he slept all day?"

"Haven't seen him, so I'm guessing he did. I wasn't going up to check."

"I'm going to go check on him."

Preach nods his head. "I'm sure he'd like that better than waking up to me."

Nico is lying diagonally across his bed, face down on his stomach. He's still wearing the trunks from the fight the afternoon before. I watch his back rise and fall. Relief floods me that he's still breathing.

Quietly, I back out of the room and pull the door shut again. I don't want to wake him after what Preach told me. I find a pen and paper in the drawer in the kitchen and leave him a note on the table. *Stopped by to check on you, didn't want to wake you. Sweet Dreams. Elle*

It's almost ten o'clock at night by the time my phone finally rings. I grab it off the end table anxiously. "Hey."

"Hey." Nico's voice is groggy and it sounds like he might have just woken up.

"Did you just wake up?" If he did, those are some powerful drugs because he would have been out for almost sixteen hours straight.

"Yeah."

"How do you feel?"

"I'm fine." Nico's inflection tells me he doesn't want to talk about it. It seems like I'll be getting answers with minimum words again.

"Is there anything I can do?"

"I said I'm fine, Elle." It's not lost on me that he uses my name. I became Babe to him the first week I met him. It shouldn't be significant, but for some reason the simple change makes me feel like we've taken a step back. And his tone, I try not to get offended. I remember people trying to help me, when I wasn't ready to accept it yet. It just pissed me off. But still, I can't help but feel disappointed that he is going to close me out with everyone else.

"Okay."

There's an uncomfortable silence that sits between us. Something

146

that I've never experienced with Nico. My stomach twists, but I wait for him to speak first.

"I need to make something to eat. I'll call you tomorrow."

I act like nothing's wrong, even though I feel my heart squeeze at his words. He's blowing me off. "Okay. I'll talk to you tomorrow." I do my best to sound upbeat when I'm anything but.

For the first time, I realize I've really fallen for Nico Hunter.

CHAPTER 35

Nico

It's fucking killing me to keep away from Elle. She's all I can think about, but I don't want her to see me this way. Weak. Scared. I can't even fight anymore. I thought I'd moved past it all, moved on with my life after more than a year of running in place. But the nightmares are back. I can't sleep and god damn Preach won't give me any more of the pills.

She knows I've been avoiding her. I'm ruining the one good thing that I've found in a very long time, because I'm afraid to close my eyes and see his face. He haunts me. Haunts me for what I did to him, but I fucking deserve it.

I'm on the other side of the gym listening to one of Preach's lectures for the hundredth time, when she walks in. I'm not expecting her, I don't hear the door open or the sound of her voice, but somehow I feel her presence. I turn around and look for her. Our eyes find each other like magnets. Fuck, she's beautiful. I love her in those god damn prissy looking suits she wears. Her face is apprehensive at first, like she's not sure if showing up unannounced is going to be welcome. Jesus, I did that to her. Made her feel that she may not be welcome. What a total asshole I am.

She smiles at me from across the room and I can't help but feel the first glimpse of light I've felt in days. I watch her as she gets closer and see her face falter when she gets a good look at me. I look like shit. I haven't shaved since before the fight and my eyes are dark from sleepless nights. I'm pretty sure I've been wearing the same shirt for at least thirty-six hours and I'm wondering if I might also smell too.

"Hi." I see the concern in her eyes when she reaches me and speaks.

"Hey."

"Figured if I didn't ask, you couldn't tell me not to come." She smiles at me apprehensively and it makes me want to reach over and kiss her so hard she'll never doubt I want her near me. But I don't. Instead I stand like an asshole and say nothing and just nod my head as if I can comprehend what is actually going on in that beautiful head of hers.

"Preach, do you mind if I steal him for a little bit?" She turns to the bastard that was chewing me out a minute ago, who is now all smiles for her.

"By all means, take him. You can keep him for all I care." The second part is mumbled under his breath as Preach walks away, but we both hear it.

"Can we go upstairs and talk?" Her voice is low, sweet.

I nod and lead the way. I pull down the gate to the elevator to my loft and suddenly it's just the two of us and the car feels small. She smells so damn good. Everything about her is good, unlike me. I hate myself for wanting her so much, even though she deserves better.

Elle puts her purse on the kitchen counter and takes a few minutes before she turns around to face me. But when she does, she looks nervous.

"I want you to talk to me. You won't let me in." Her voice is shaky, but when I look at her she squares her shoulders and digs deep for whatever she is working towards.

"I don't want to talk Elle." What does she want me to tell her? That I need time to sort out the demons in my head? The demons that I deserve to haunt me every hour of every day for the rest of my life?

She takes two steps toward me, stopping just in front of me. "I can help… and there's grief counseling…and groups to help people going through things like this."

My response is a sardonic laugh and I can see immediately it's the wrong reaction. Elle's face quickly changes from concerned to pissed off. She crosses her arms in front of her chest and it looks like she is ready for a fight.

"You think it's funny that I want to help?"

"No I think it's funny that you think you can help."

"I can help. But you have to let me."

"Elle, run while you have the chance. You can't fix me. I'm not some project for you to take on like charity. You're better off with someone who is more like you."

Here eyes widen to saucers. "More like me? What does that mean? William? Is that what you're telling me, I should go back to someone like William?" Her voice is growing louder with each response.

The mention of William's name from Elle's lips strikes me harder than any physical blow. The thought of that pretty boy anywhere near my Elle makes me froth at the mouth. I'm angry. Angry at just hearing her say the words. But maybe that's really where she belongs.

"You want William, Elle?" Seething, the words make me sick to even her myself say them.

"I want you. I want to help you, damn it!"

"You can't help me, Elle. I'm fucking broken. I killed a man. With my own two hands, I took another person's life. Only a monster does that. A monster that will rot in hell. It's where I fucking belong!"

"It was an accident!" We are screaming at each other now. Completely and totally screaming at the top of our lungs, each trying to get our point across by yelling louder.

"It was my hand that dealt him what killed him. That's not an accident, it's murder. And murderers are unredeemable."

Elle looks up at me and she's pale as a ghost. For a second I think she might pass out.

"You really think there's no forgiveness in what happened?" She's no longer yelling, her voice is low and breaks mid-sentence.

"Forgiveness from who, Elle? The only person that could grant me absolution is dead."

Tears are streaming down her face as she runs out of my loft and rips the elevator door down. I watch as she frantically presses the button to make her escape. She's desperate to get away from me, and I don't blame her one bit.

CHAPTER 36

Elle

I have no idea how I even made it home. The tears blurred my vision so badly, I could barely see. Panic seizes me as I think about how much worse it could have been. The only saving grace is that I never got to carry out my plan to tell Nico why I can help him, what makes me so uniquely qualified to understand what he is going through. I sob as I recall his words over and over in my head, *"It was my hand that dealt him what killed him. That's not an accident, it's murder. And murderers are unredeemable."*

I don't know why I thought we were the same. We're not. I'm so much worse. Yet, he thinks *he's* a monster for what he did...and what happened to him was truly an accident. Unlike me. I'm the one who is unredeemable. If he hates himself so much for what he did when he didn't intend for it to happen, what would he think when he found out about me? Mine wasn't an accident.

I've suppressed emotions for so long, that it's like a dam breaking when the tears start to come. They flood me like raging waters. Uncontrollably, I cry and cry until I finally feel like I'm drowning and sleep takes me as I surrender, my mind hoping to find peace at rest.

"You stupid whore. I told you not to go running to your sister's house again." My father grabs a fistful of my mother's hair and yanks with all his might, sending my already frail mother across the room. The pot on the stove makes a loud clank as she hits into the stove. My mother's face is already black

and blue from last time and her nose is probably broken. Although she can't be sure since she stopped going to the doctor a few years ago. Doctors ask too many questions.

"Did you think I wouldn't find you, you worthless cunt? I'll always find you. When are you going to learn your fucking lesson?" My father takes two long strides toward my mother and she folds her body into a ball to protect herself, bracing for what she knows is inevitable. I watch as he rears his leg back and kicks her in the side with all his might. Her body falls to the side, but she's still huddled into a ball, her tiny arms straining to cover her own head.

It's not difficult for my father to lift my mother, he's six feet tall and well over two hundred pounds and she's tiny. The last year has been so bad that she keeps getting tinier. She thinks I don't notice, but I do. Her clothes are all too big and she barely eats anymore. She's always sad lately.

He reaches down and grabs her off the floor by her neck, lifting her upright and off her feet in one swift motion. Even when he's this drunk, it doesn't seem to lessen his strength. Sometimes I think it gives him more. More power. More hatred. The evil that's always lurking in the depths finds its way to the surface and then it's even worse. Almost as if the evil gets bottled up so long that it explodes when it finally comes out.

It wasn't always like this. My father wasn't always the monster he is today. I remember him coming home after work and sitting on the couch. He would playfully pull my mother onto his lap when she came to bring him a drink. She would giggle and they would kiss. I thought it was gross. But I'd give anything to go back to those days now. We were happy. And he wasn't drunk and angry all the time.

But then things changed. He lost his business and we had to move. Move out of our big house with the pretty green lawn and into a small apartment with a concrete patch for a yard. My father hated to move, it made him really angry. At first he would just yell a lot. And drink. He started to drink a lot. Sometimes I would get up for school and he'd have liquor in his coffee mug instead of coffee.

Then one night mom burned dinner while she was trying to give me a bath at the same time. And when Dad saw the mess, he smacked her across the face. Hard. I remember him telling her she was wasting his money. She cried and apologized. The next morning he was still passed out. Mom told me Dad was under a lot of stress and he didn't mean to hurt her. It was just an accident.

But then it happened again. And again. And again. And the hitting got worse. The smacks turned into punches and punches turned into kicks. Until it got to the point where he was beating her almost every day. She almost always has bruises and she didn't go out much anymore. We tried to leave a few times. But he always found us and brought us back. He would apologize and say it would never happen again. Then when we went home, it usually got worse. Like this time.

Mom's feet are dangling and her face is turning bright red. I'm afraid and I don't know what to do. He really may kill her this time. "Stop! Stop! You're going to kill her." Desperately, I beg my father. Tears are streaming down my face as I grab his arm, frantic to get my mother air. He swats me away and I go flying through the air, but at least I've managed to make him release his death grip on her throat.

My mom falls to the floor, her hands holding her neck as she gasps for air. She's making a loud wheezing noise with each breath as she tries frantically to bring air into her lungs. My father turns and looks at me, sitting where I've landed after his push. His eyes are dark and crazy and I begin to tremble. I've never been so scared. He's going to kill us. Both of us. I can see it in his eyes. Whatever semblance of a man that remained from what used to be my father is gone. A monster has replaced him.

I think he's going to come after me, but then he turns. His focus back to my mother, still gasping for air desperately on the floor. With one arm he grabs her hair in his fist and hoists her back up, slamming her into the refrigerator. Everything resting on the top falls, some of it landing on my mother. But it doesn't distract him. Holding her head steady with a fistful of hair against the refrigerator he leans his head into my mother's, his once handsome face contorting to the point that he no longer even resembles himself. "What did I tell you I would do if you tried to leave again, you stupid little cunt? This is all your fault. You bring it all on yourself, you worthless whore. You're garbage."

Then he pulls his face back and winds up before slamming his fist square into her cheek. I hear a loud crack and I'm not sure if it's my mother's face or my father's hand, but the sound makes me sick. Physically. I vomit all over myself.

My father punches her again and this time there's no crack. All I hear is a noise that sounds like a seal barking. It's my mother, she's crying out in pain, but her voice is still gone from when he choked her. It's a horrible sound. A horrible, horrible sickening sound. She can't breathe and the sound is getting more desperate, but lower at the same time. Like she's running out of time. She gasps again and I hear that sound again. It's the most horrible noise I've ever heard in my life. It's also the last thing I remember until the gun blast jolts me.

I tried for months to remember what happened. I remember the sound, my mother trying to breathe. Then I remember the gunshot. It was so loud it hurt my ears. The ringing won't stop. I remember watching my father fall and seeing blood start to pour out of his head. There was a lot of blood. More than I've watched my mother clean up of her own blood after the beatings. It pools into a circle that just keeps getting bigger and bigger. Then the pool reaches me and it starts to seep onto my bare feet. But I don't move. I have no idea where the gunshot came from. Until I look down and realize I'm holding the gun in my own hands.

I wake up holding my ears. For a long moment I can actually hear the ringing. It's exactly the same as that day. Only when I sit up the sound disappears and the room is silent. Eerily silent. I slap my hands together just to hear sound. I need to be sure I'm awake and the monster is really gone.

CHAPTER 37

Nico

It's been three days and Elle still won't answer my calls. I know I fucked up, and I'll understand if she never wants to see me again, but I need to see her. Need to apologize for how I treated her. She only wanted to help me, and I was too busy wallowing in self-pity to accept it. I'm a total asshole.

I've called and texted. The flowers that I tried to have delivered were returned to the shop twice because no one answered. I banged on her door myself, apologizing and asking her to give me just two minutes. Either she wasn't home or she hates me so much she won't even waste her breath to blow me off.

Swallowing my pride, I finally head to her office. I just need to see her. I promise myself that I won't make a scene.

"Hi Regina." I try to sound casual, instead of the desperate loser that I really am.

"Hi Nico."

I can tell by her face that she knows something happened. She tries to smile, but she looks sad.

"Is Elle around?" I glance over Regina's shoulder, hoping to catch sight of her.

"No, I'm sorry, she's not."

Fuck casual. I'm desperate. "Please Regina. If she told you to tell me she isn't here, go tell her I need to see her."

There's something I think might be pity in Regina's face when she responds. "She's really not here. She took a few days off."

"Is she okay?"

"I think so. She just needs some time. There's a lot you don't understand."

"I'm in love with her Regina. I need to see her. Tell her I'm sorry." Until the words come out of my mouth, I hadn't even admitted it to myself. But damn it, it doesn't even scare me. I need to fix this. My own shit isn't even important anymore. I just need to get to Elle.

Regina looks into my eyes, assessing my sincerity. She looks conflicted, but then I see her smile and shake her head. "She's going to kick my ass for this. But, here." She scribbles something on paper and offers it to me. "Her stepfather has a cabin out in Spring Grove. I'm supposed to head there after work." I go to take the paper from her hand, but she pulls it back and looks up at me. "You have until midnight. If she doesn't text me not to come by then, I'm coming and you are leaving. Got it?"

"Got it." I'd make a deal with the devil to get that paper from her hand.

I make the three hour drive in just under two and a half hours. The house is in the middle of nowhere, on a big lake. It bothers me that she's up here all by herself. The closest house is probably at least a mile away. The inside door is wide open, only a screen door keeping out the unwelcomed.

I knock and feel more alive than I have in days when she responds. Just hearing her voice brings me a sense of relief. She yells from somewhere in the distance. She thinks I'm Regina. "What are you knocking for? Come in."

I open the door and step inside, looking around.

"Was Lawrence pissed I didn't come in again?" Her voice is coming from the back of the house somewhere, but it's getting closer. "Was the drive…"

She finally rounds a corner and stops in her tracks when she sees me.

"What are you doing here?"

"I talked Regina into giving me the address."

"But…why?"

Hesitantly, I take steps in her direction. She doesn't move toward me, but at least she isn't running the other way either. I stop when I get in front of her. She isn't wearing any makeup and it looks like she's been crying recently. I'm such a complete asshole.

"I wanted to tell you I'm sorry."

Elle says nothing, she's waiting for me to continue. "I was out of line the other night. You were trying to help, and I was…a total asshole to you."

She half-heartedly smiles at me and nods her head. "It's okay. I get it. You were upset. I shouldn't have pushed."

I should be happy at hearing her say she forgives me, but it's what she's not saying that gives me a hollow feeling in the pit of my stomach.

"Will you give me a chance to make it up to you?" I reach out for her hand. She looks at my hand and then up to my eyes, but she doesn't give me the hand I am reaching for like a lifeline as I begin to feel myself sink.

"I'm not mad at you, Nico. But I thought about some of the things you said. And you're right. We're just too different."

My heartbeat pounds in my chest. I forgot that I had told her she was better off with someone more like her. Fucking William. That was her response. I want to break that stuffy asshole in two. I can't even look at her. I need to get out with at least my dignity intact. At least she let me say my piece.

"Okay, Elle." She doesn't try to stop me as I turn and make my way to the door.

CHAPTER 38

Elle

The next morning I find Regina sleeping on the couch. Traitor. She wakes as I'm making breakfast. Okay, so maybe she didn't wake, but instead I woke her up by slamming all the pots and pans I took out. Some of them didn't actually need to be taken out of the cabinet. But those just looked extra loud.

"I take it you hate me this morning?" Regina walks into the kitchen rubbing her eyes. "I'm sorry. He looked so sad and, I thought…thought maybe there was a chance you could work it out."

"Did you not hear what I told you? He thinks I'm a monster. An unredeemable monster. And he's right."

"He said *he* was a monster."

"Only because he doesn't know who I am. And we're keeping it that way." I look over at Regina for confirmation and she doesn't look firm on her answer. "Right, Regina?"

My best friend makes a growl of frustration in response before I hear the words I need to hear. "Of course, you know I would never tell your secrets."

Regina is my most trustworthy friend, yet I'm a little relieved to hear her recommit to our vow of secrecy. She has a soft spot for Nico Hunter.

The next week passes in a blur. I work twelve hours a day for seven days straight to catch up from the three days I spent wallowing in my self-pity. There's always plenty of work to do at my small firm, but ninety hours in a week isn't really necessary and I know it. But I need to keep myself busy. I hate going home. There's nothing to do but think. Think about a man that made my steady, even-keeled life into a roller coaster. A roller coaster of emotions that I had forgot I was capable of experiencing.

My life was simple before Nico Hunter walked into it. A good job, a nice guy to date, and no more nightmares. For ten years I managed to keep my life steady. I existed. Then he walked in and suddenly existing wasn't enough anymore. And I wanted it. I wanted to stop existing and start living. Finally. But I should have known it wouldn't work. Even at my weekly support group, I watched as people's faces changed once they heard my story.

It's Thursday evening and I'm late for meeting William. We're meeting a client we share at a restaurant. It's the last place Nico and I had dinner and just walking in stirs my emotions. The slightest reminder is all it takes.

William waves to me from the bar when I walk in. He's not seated at a table like he normally is when he waits for me because I'm late.

"Hey." I look around for our client. "Is Mr. Munley later than me?"

William stands and kisses me on the cheek and smiles. "He's not coming till seven."

"Oh, I thought it was six."

William sips his drink. "That's because I told you six."

I look at him confused, although I really have no right to be. He continues, "Munley doesn't like to be kept waiting, so I told you six and him seven, so he wouldn't be kept waiting." William grins.

I'm surprised, but I shouldn't be. I smile at William and pretend to be offended. "Are you accusing me of being perpetually late?"

"In all the years we've known each other, I don't think you've ever once been on time. You're forgetting how we met. I was the one that let you copy my notes when you walked in a half hour late to class every day."

He's teasing me, but he's right. The only time I can even recall being on time was when I went to see Nico. I couldn't wait to get to him. The thought brings my mood down.

For the next twenty minutes William and I catch up on clients. We haven't really spent much time together since the night Nico and I got together and I realize that I really do miss the familiarity. We slip easily into our roles and our conversation is light and steady, almost as if we pick up exactly where we left off. My mood lightens, slightly.

Then something changes in the air. It's a feeling that speeds my heart and makes my palms sweaty and I look around to see if it's just me or if everyone else seems to notice it too. And then I see him. He's twenty feet away and staring daggers at me. My breath catches when our eyes meet and I see that look in his eyes. He's angry and wild and my traitorous body responds to him, even though I'm obviously the last thing he wants to see.

We stare at each other for a solid minute. Neither of us attempts to close the distance between us and we don't say a word. When Nico's eyes finally release mine, I watch as they go from me to William and back to me. Then he turns and walks out of the restaurant, and for a second I think I've imagined the whole thing.

"I take it you two aren't seeing each other anymore?" William's words confirm my vision was reality and not in my head.

I force myself to return my attention to William and shake my head no. I can't even say the words out loud. Although I'm facing him, I'm too lost in my thoughts for the small smile that appears for a split second on William's face to register meaning in my brain.

I'm under a cloud of haze all during dinner. Luckily William takes the lead and I don't think our client even notices. I try to participate in the conversation, but I find my thoughts running away with themselves, and they all lead back to one place. Nico Hunter.

CHAPTER 39

Nico

I can actually see that douchebag lawyer's face on the bag as I pummel it. He's fucking lucky I didn't drag his pansy ass back here and hang him from the chain instead.

"You gonna stop acting like a spoiled brat and go after your girl?" Preach is lucky he's old or I'd kick his ass too.

"She's not my girl anymore." I hit the bag hard with a left and then a quick right. My knuckle pops out of place, but the pain feels too good to stop.

"Maybe you've grown soft." Preach stands behind the bag as he speaks. Smart move.

I stop hitting to respond. "She doesn't want to see me anymore. How does that make me soft?" My words are angry, bordering on violent, and my fists are at my sides clenched tightly. But Preach doesn't flinch. The old man has balls of steel.

"The Nico I know is a fighter. Isn't she worth the fight?" Preach hits me with his last verbal jab and walks away.

My mind is swimming in thoughts as I shower. I feel like I might explode. Seeing her tonight fucked with my head. For a second, I thought there was a chance. Why else would Regina have told me to go to the restaurant? Does she want to see me beat the crap out of William? And I could have sworn that there was something in Elle's eyes when she saw me too. But she stayed put...next to *him*....and let me walk out the door again. *Let me.* Fuck, Preach is right, I am being a damn pussy. I'm done letting her make the decisions. She's worth it... worth the fight.

It's almost midnight when I arrive at her door. If that asshole is inside, I'm afraid what I might do. But I'm done keeping on the sidelines. I have a lot of baggage that she doesn't deserve, but I can carry it for the both of us. I'm not going down without a fight. I knock and wait.

After a few minutes, the door opens and I'm relieved to see it looks like she's been sleeping. She looks at me and for a minute we just stand there, neither of us saying a word. Then I catch it. It's the difference between a good fighter and a great fighter. Reading your opponents eyes and finding an opening. And going for it. So I do. I go for it.

CHAPTER 40

Elle

For a second I think I must be dreaming. He's so beautiful standing there, a perfect male specimen. I just want to fall into his strong arms and let him block everything else out for me for a little while. It's selfish to want him and I know it. But suddenly my heartbeat is thundering in my chest and every hair on my body is back on alert.

Neither of us says anything for a minute. Then he comes to me. And I think he's going to kiss me, but instead he reaches down and lifts me into his arms, cradling me as he walks into my apartment and kicks the door shut behind him.

He doesn't stop moving or put me down until we reach my bedroom. He gently lays me down on the end of the bed. Our eyes locked as he stands over me. I want to touch his jaw. Run my finger over the squareness of it and feel the stubble prickle beneath my finger. His pale green eyes watch me. Watch me take him in. Greedily, I let my eyes soak up every ounce. From head to toe I devour him. My body aches for him to touch me. Be inside of me again.

When my eyes reach his again, the paleness is replaced with a stormy grey. There's a huge knot in my throat. It's blocking the passage of my tears that I'm holding back. I'm afraid to speak for fear that the dam will open again and this time I won't be able to swim to the surface for air, I'll drown in my own tears.

Nico slowly leans down, his eyes never leaving mine as he comes to rest on top of me. One hand on either side of my head, he keeps his head pulled back so we can see each other, but his body fully is covering mine. I could no longer move, even if I wanted to. But I don't want to anyway. God I missed him. The rock hard feel of his body against my soft curves. Being underneath the sheer power of the man.

"Mine." It's the first word he says to me, and the last before his lips crash down on me in the most wildly, sensual, seductive, possessive kiss I've ever had. One of his hands snakes around the back of my neck and he pulls me tighter to him. I feel the inexplicable need to chase away every single molecule that is between us, until there's nothing left but me and him. Being held together tighter than I've ever been held isn't good enough. I need him inside of me. To be part of me. To be one indivisible body that shares the breath that fills both our lungs.

We're both panting as we come up for air, our mouths still pressed tightly against each other. Neither one of us willing to release the other first. "Mine," Nico repeats the word with a growl. The words vibrate on my lips and I feel it shoot all the way down to the already swollen flesh between my legs.

"Yours." I respond breathlessly.

And then it's a frantic race to get our clothes off. Nico lifts his hips only enough to somehow maneuver his pants off. Mine he has even less trouble dispensing with. I feel the thick, hard length of him against my bare skin and it makes me shiver with anticipation. I feel my own wetness between my legs, my body ready to take him in even before my mind catches up to it.

Pushing up from the bed at the hips, I tilt upwards the little bit that I can move underneath him, silently urging him to take me. I need him now. Right now.

"Say it again."

I know what he wants to hear. "Yours." I whisper quietly as I take his face in my hands and he responds by pushing inside of me. Hard. And deep. His mouth covers mine again, as he stifles my moan with a gentle kiss that contradicts the harshness of his thrust.

He releases my mouth as he stills deep inside of me. "Again."

"Yours."

Nico pulls his hips back and thrusts into me again even harder. He stretches me wide and again settles between my legs. He doesn't say anything when he stills, but there's no doubt what he's waiting for.

"Yours."

After a few more deep thrusts that are rewarded with the word he needs to hear, Nico takes my hands and clasps them together, bringing them up and over my head. He holds both my hands in one of his and pulls almost all the way out from inside of me, lifting his body off of mine. I watch as he stops to look down at me. He's positioned me how he wants me and now he's admiring his work. My hands secured tightly over my head and my legs spread wide for him, I'm completely and utterly exposed. He doesn't ask me to say the word again. He doesn't need too. He sees it laying out before his eyes.

He closes his eyes and takes a deep breath. For a second he looks peaceful. But then he begins to pound into me. Each thrust deeper and faster than the one before. Our bodies are covered in sweat and each thrust down makes a smacking noise as our bodies slap against each other in fury.

Nico grunts on every plunge down and I cry out on every slippery stroke upward as we find our rhythm together. Instinctively, I try to move to reach out and touch him, but his grip holding my hands above my head tightens, keeping me in place. I feel possessed, completely and totally possessed by this man. And it's that feeling that sends me over the edge.

I moan through my orgasm, unashamed by what I feel. What he makes me feel. Nico's body tightens in response to my orgasm and the heat of his semen pouring into me extends my own release. Together we furiously give ourselves over to the pleasures of our bodies; loud, obscene sounds coming from both of us as we both realize we are climaxing together.

I wake in the morning to a warm hand tracing the curve of my spine up my back slowly as I lie naked on my stomach. I wiggle a bit as he reaches the top of my ass, his thick fingers halting only for a second before they continue their assault downward, gently pushing their way in between my ass cheeks, tracing the outline of my most private areas. A little giggle comes out when he continues his tracing underneath me, finding my still swollen clit.

"Shh." Nico's voice is gentle now. So different from the demanding man who came to me in the middle of the night to stake his claim. He leans over my back and gently kisses the back of my neck, leaving a sweet trail of wet from the nape of my neck up to my ear. "I want you." His voice is low and throaty in my ear and it sounds incredibly erotic.

"So take me." I whisper on a small moan as his teeth sink into my ear.

"No. I want you to give yourself to me. I want *you*, Elle. *All of you.*"

I turn over to face him and it's like the first time I've ever seen him, even though we only fell asleep a few hours ago. His hair is disheveled and he has the start of a five o'clock shadow on his masculine jaw. The vision steals my breath away. I reach up and cup his jaw in my hand, my thumb stroking his cheek where I know a dimple hides just beneath the surface.

Our eyes meet and I realize he's serious. He's not being playful. He wants me to give myself to him and not just in the bed right now. "I want to… but I'm not sure I can." I respond with honesty.

Nico shuts his eyes and I think I've hurt him again. I can't stand to hurt this man anymore. But then he opens them and surprises me. "We'll work on it. Together."

A lone tear escapes my eye and Nico brushes it away before I give myself to him, in the only way I can at the moment. And he takes what I give him, making love to me sweetly when I need it most.

We don't get out of bed all day, making up for lost time. I missed these quiet moments when we just lay in bed, my head tucked into the crook of his broad shoulder, him stroking my hair with his big hand so gently. I run my finger up and down his breastbone, mindlessly feeling the bumps and curves of the walls of his thick muscles along the way. I'm happy, but there's a gnawing feeling lurking just beneath my contentment. I know there are things we have to talk about, things that will ruin everything. But I just want to stay in the here and now for a little while longer. I love the way he looks at me, selfishly I don't want it to change. But I know it will when he finds out.

Sensing my distance, Nico lifts my chin upward to look at him in the eyes. "I'm sorry, Babe. I know we still need to talk."

I panic, desperate to just be us a while longer. "You need to feed me first." I give him a wry grin. As if on cue, Nico's stomach growls, and just like that I get a reprieve. At least for a little while.

As usual, Nico lifts me and seats me on the counter while he cooks. I'm wearing his shirt and watching the sinfully sexy man walk around my kitchen in only his jeans, the top button of which is still open. He's a walking paradox with the ripped muscles of his chest exposed as he moves around the kitchen barefoot, almost gracefully, tossing eggs into a bowl to whip with some other stuff I didn't even know I had in my fridge. He passes me on his way to the stove and plants a chaste kiss on my lips. Delicious.

We both devour everything on our plates. I hadn't really even realized how hungry I was until the food was right in front of me. Everything Nico has cooked me has been better than a restaurant would serve. I'm really not quite sure if my opinion is just that biased about anything related to Nico Hunter, or if he's that great of a cook. But I don't really care. I'd take the sight of him cooking with no shirt on in my kitchen every day, even if the food tasted putrid.

I tell Nico to relax and begin to clear our plates and load the dishwasher, but he helps me anyway. "You cooked, you don't have to help me clean up." I smile at him. "Besides, it's the only thing I'm good at in the kitchen."

Nico comes behind me as I load our plates into the dishwasher and bends down to kiss the back of my neck softly. "But the sooner we get cleaned up." His words trail off as he runs kisses down my neck and over to my left shoulder. I let my eyes drift closed and enjoy the moment. When he finally continues his thought his voice is lower and velvety. "The sooner we can get our talk over with and get back into bed."

My eyes flash back open and reality comes crashing in as my stomach drops. There have been days, even months, filled with regret over the sins of my past, but I've never hated the man that ruined my life more than I do right at this moment. I don't blame myself anymore. I blame him. Blame him for everything that happened before and the years he took from me as I struggled to get my life back after. But I've never hated him more than I hate him right now, because he is about to take yet another part of my life away. The way that Nico looks at me.

I can't stall any longer. I think of what my therapist would tell me to do if she was sitting right next to me, watching me act like a coward. She'd say rip the Band-Aid off. Allow the wound to breathe...to heal itself. The worst part is the anticipation of the tear, not the tear itself.

So I take a deep breath and quietly lead Nico to the couch. He sits and pulls me on top of him, one leg on each side of his thighs, straddling him on his lap. I can't have this conversation while I'm this close. I need distance. I begin to lift onto one leg, attempting to reposition myself off of him, but Nico firms his grip on my hips.

I look up at him confused. "I...I'm just moving..."

"I know what you're doing."

My face must show my confusion, because Nico doesn't wait for me to respond.

"I want to talk right here."

"Why?" Truly, I'm confused by his action...refusing to allow me to put space between us.

"Because it's harder for you to avoid me when I'm right in your face."

And I thought I was doing such a good job of ducking our conversation.

I shut my eyes and take a long deep breath in. When I open them, Nico's watching me intently and it makes it that much harder. But I need to do it. I rip the Band-Aid off and show him my wounds. The horrific wounds I've been carrying around, alone, for more than half of my life.

"My father was abusive." My words are low, but I'm steady. I can do this. I look down at Nico's bare chest as I speak and find a tiny dot of a freckle just to the right of his belly button. It's so small I hadn't noticed it before. But now it's all I can focus on. My eyes are glued to it. Nico's hands on my hips grow tighter. I'm not sure if he thinks I'm going to bolt or if he unconsciously does it in response to the start of my story, but either way somehow it helps me. Just knowing he is holding me tight gives me the strength to continue.

"Not me. Just my mother. It went on for years. Sometimes we would leave, but he would find us and everything would be okay for a little while. But then it would start again." I rub my pointer finger over the little freckle, the slow back and forth motion soothes me. When I was a kid and my father would start in on my mother, I would sit on my bed and rock. Rock back and forth. Somehow it calmed me.

Nico doesn't say anything, he just keeps his strong hold on me and sits quietly. Waiting and listening. "It got bad. One night he beat her so bad that she didn't get out of bed for more than three weeks. Her nose was broken and both eyes were so swollen shut that she would flinch when I would come into her bedroom, because she couldn't be sure if it was me or if it was him." My voice cracks, but I don't cry. I just wish I could tell the story without reliving the picture in my head. The few times I've told the story out loud, it's always the same. I'm back there and I'm narrating what I see in my head, giving the play-by-play, as if the little girl isn't even me.

"On the twenty-third day, she got out of bed. The bruises were starting to heal and her face was mostly grey and yellow. The swelling had gone down too. She stood in the kitchen and made me a can of soup. It was Campbell's. Chicken and Rice. She put it in the brown and white striped croc bowl that I loved to eat out of. I remember thinking it was the best thing I ever ate."

I quiet for a minute as I watch my mother and I sit at the table and eat soup together. It plays out in my head as if it was really right in front of me. She smiled at me and I smiled back. It didn't make things all better, but I remember thinking we were going to be okay. I had a strange feeling of relief as we sat there and ate in silence. For three weeks I must have been walking around with my shoulders feeling tense, but I didn't realize it until I felt them ease as we finished our soup.

My shoulders relax a little. Then I take a deep breath, knowing what would come next. "Then he came home. We were still sitting at the table, our soup bowls still in front of us when he stumbled in. Drunk. He was always drunk. And angry."

I close my eyes and fight back my tears. I know what comes next, I've seen it in my head a thousand times, but each time it's as hard to watch as the first. It never gets any easier. I'm not sure how long I sit there in silence, willing my tears away. I don't even realize I've stopped speaking and gone somewhere else until I hear Nico's voice.

"You don't have to, Elle. Just let me hold you and forget the past." His voice is gentle and kind and caring and it takes every ounce of strength in my body not to give in and just let him hold me. Take care of me and make it all go away. But I can't. I need to rip the Band-Aid off.

172

My mind back in the present, I find the freckle and reclaim it as my focus, continuing with what I have to say. What I need to say. "He almost killed her that night. He lifted her by her throat and crushed her windpipe. She couldn't breathe. But that wasn't good enough. He wouldn't stop." The tears start to flow from my eyes, but I won't let them keep me from what I need to do. "He wouldn't stop. He just hit her over and over again. And she made this noise. This horrible noise because she couldn't breathe. She was gasping for air, fighting with what little she had left." The tears turn into sobs and I feel my body trembling.

"Come here, Baby." Nico tries to pull me to him, but I won't allow it. I need to get it all out.

For the first time since I started speaking, I look up at Nico. His eyes are pained and filled with unshed tears of his own as he watches me cry and listens to my story. I take one more deep breath and look into his eyes when I speak, my words coming out quiet, but their meaning unmistakably clear. "I killed him. I knew where his gun was hidden and I shot him." Nico's eyes widen, he wasn't expecting what I told him. "That's why I know." My voice is barely a whisper. "I know what you feel like."

I cry until there are no more tears left. I don't know how much time passes, but Nico holds me tight until my body is wrenched of every last sob and tear. And I let him. For the first time in my life, I let someone else hold it, even if it's just for a little while. He holds the pain and the guilt and the burden, all of it. And with the weight lifted from me, I fall asleep. Sound asleep.

CHAPTER 41

Nico

Elle shifts in her sleep and I tighten my grip. She hasn't budged in hours, not since she fell asleep in my arms. I eased my back down onto the couch and laid her out on top of me while I held her. My arms are numb from holding her so tight, but there is no way I'm letting go. Not ever.

I thought I understood what it meant to feel pain, but I had no god damn clue until I saw her face. Seeing her pain made anything I've went through pale in comparison. Worse than a blow to the chest, the pain is physical and emotional. The urge to hit something is almost unbearable. How could any human being do that to a woman, no less in front of a little girl? Forcing a twelve-year-old to defend her own mother at the cost of taking her own father's life. No, not her father's life. She took the life of a monster, who deserved it. I only wish it was me. Wish I could take it all away and let it be me who went through it, not Elle.

She looks so peaceful when she sleeps. I'm pissed off at myself for not being there for her when it happened. Deep down I know it's irrational to hate myself for not protecting her when I hadn't even met her yet...but it doesn't make the feeling go away just because common sense tells me it's impossible.

When I froze in the cage and beat myself up over it, this little angel reaches out to help me, knowing that it will only bring bad shit to the surface again for her. And what do I do when she puts herself out there for me? I basically turn my back on her. I'm so fucking self-centered… so worried about myself that I make her retreat. It must have taken everything she had to reach out and try to help me with what she bears herself. I'm a total asshole.

CHAPTER 42

Elle

I'm confused when I wake up. I don't even remember falling asleep. But I'm lying on top of Nico and he's holding me so tight that for a minute I forget what happened last night. I told him. And now he'll never look at me the same. Even my therapist and friends I met in group change when they hear my story. Everyone except Regina. She understands me because she has her own cross to bear. Some look at me with pity, others think I'm a monster...that there is no justification for taking another life. I know what they think.

I have no idea what time it is, but the sun isn't peaking in through the window yet, so it must not be morning. I try to close my eyes and force myself back to sleep, but my bladder has other plans for us. I attempt to gently slip out of Nico's arms as he sleeps, but his arms tighten around me and pull me back into place.

"Where do you think you're going?" His voice takes me by surprise, I thought he was sleeping.

"I have to go to the bathroom." I respond to his chest, I'm not ready to see his beautiful green eyes. The ones that used to look at me like I was special, like he wanted to devour me.

Nico's grip loosens and I quietly get up without another word and make my way to the bathroom. I'm horrified when I look in the mirror. My face is all puffy, blotchy, and red and there are black streaks of makeup dried on both cheeks. My hair is a tangled mess on one side and the other side looks as if it was glued to my face. Wonderful.

I wash up and do my best to look presentable, but there's not much to help a swollen face except time…and maybe some ice. I make my way back to the couch in the dark where I expect to find Nico, but he isn't there. For a second I panic and think he's already left me, but then I hear him walking behind me.

"Bath or bed? I feel like I'm gonna break that little girly couch you have every time I move an inch." He wraps his arms around my waist from behind as he speaks and it takes me a minute to realize what he's asking.

"Bed."

I'm thankful that we manage to make it to the bedroom without turning on any lights, I'm not ready to see his eyes. I'm not sure I'll ever be ready, but I'm being selfish and just want to pretend nothing's changed a little while longer. Nico waits until after I'm in bed before climbing in and then he climbs in next to me. Lying on his side, he wraps his arm around my waist as I lie on my back and he pulls me so I'm lying next to him. His big hand reaches up and pushes the hair that's already fallen out of the hair tie I had just secured out of my face. He rubs his thumb up and down the side of my cheek and my eyes close, relaxing at his touch, so gentle and soothing.

"You okay?"

I think before I speak. "Not really."

I can't really see his face, but I feel him nod once, accepting my response.

A long moment of silence passes before Nico speaks again. "What are you most afraid of right now?"

I know the answer right away, but I think about how to respond to the question anyway. I don't try to catch the few tears that roll down my face, hoping he won't notice in the dark. But Nico's thumb catches my tears.

I still haven't summoned the courage to answer his question, when he speaks again. "I'm afraid I'm not good enough for you. That I'll drag you down into the hell that I belong in with me."

The few tears that had escaped become the eye of the storm and suddenly the torrential downpour hits and I can't stop them. But I force myself to answer through them. "I'm afraid to see the way that you'll look at me…now that you know who I really am."

Nico pulls me to him and wraps me tightly in his arms. I cry…really cry, feeling years of pent-up tears flow from my body. It's exhausting and strangely freeing at the same time. He doesn't loosen his grip on me until I have nothing left.

Eventually my breathing calms and the tears are all gone. I begin to drift off to sleep, but then suddenly it's light and I have to force my eyes closed to ward out the stream of brightness. Nico turned on the light.

"What are you doing?" My eyelids are still pressed tightly closed as I speak.

"Open your eyes." Nico's voice is soft, but his words are a command, not a question.

I don't respond, and I also don't open my eyes.

"Elle, baby, open your eyes."

His tone is so sweet, I'd find it hard to deny him anything when he talks to me like that. So I do it. I open my eyes a little and look up at him. His beautiful green eyes are right there, so close to me. And they're waiting. Waiting for me to look back at him fully. I allow it, allow my eyes to fully open and look into Nico's. At first I'm just looking at the eyes themselves. The beautiful color, the dark pupil in the sea of soft green, the thick dark eyelashes that frame the beauty God has given the man. But then I find myself looking past the surface and I'm searching. Searching for what I expect to find there. Then I realize. It's not there. No pity, no shame, no doubt. And my eyes widen when it hits me.

"There she is." The corner of Nico's mouth twitches and I can't help but smile back at him. My body heaves a deep breath of relief and I feel as though I'm at peace for the first time in a very long time. It might even be the first time I've ever felt this way.

We spend the next few hours talking and making love and I never want it to end. But I have an early afternoon deposition that I'm not prepared for and I have to drag myself into the office. "I have to get to work. I'm late, even for me."

"You're usually late to work?" Nico seems surprised.

I laugh at his comment, he must be the only person on the planet that doesn't know about my issue with timeliness. "I'm late for everything."

Nico shrugs, "I guess I didn't notice."

I smile at him and yes, I think I might even blush a little. Blush at the man who has touched every part of my body with his mouth and now knows my innermost, darkest secrets. "You seem to be the only thing that I can make it on time for."

Nico's eyebrows arch in surprise, but then a slow, smug smile spreads across his handsome face and I'm rewarded with his dimples.

I playfully smack him on his chest. "Don't get too full of yourself, I'm sure it was beginner's luck and you'll be waiting for me most of the time, just like everyone else." I attempt to leave the bed. I need to take a shower and get to work, but Nico pulls me back down and I'm quickly positioned underneath him.

I think he's still being playful, but when I look up at him, I find his face serious. "I need to know something, Elle."

"What?" I'm confused at how we went from playful to serious and what is bothering him.

"Dinner with the pansy ass last night?"

"The pansy ass?" My brows furrow as I speak... for a second I really am confused as to what he is referring to, but then I realize he means William.

Nico doesn't say anything else, he waits for my response.

"We had a business dinner with a client."

"I didn't see any client and it didn't look like business to me."

"That's because he told me the dinner was at six and not seven so that I wouldn't be late. So when I got there at six thirty, we had a half an hour to wait for our client together."

My answer seems to satisfy him, but the tension I see flee from his face only disappears for a few seconds. Then it's back.

"I don't like seeing the two of you looking so cozy."

"We're friends...we've been friends since law school."

"Men who sleep with a woman don't do friends, Babe."

"Well William does."

"I see the way he looks at you. He doesn't want to be your friend."

"Whatever." I roll my eyes, this conversation is going nowhere. "It's not like I have a choice, we have cases together."

"Okay, so you work together. You don't need to sit at a bar and have drinks too."

"You don't understand." I'm sure that he just doesn't get what William and I have. William's fine with being friends and I don't understand why he's acting jealous.

Nico releases me and I think our conversation is over, so I begin to walk to the door, intent to take a shower and finally drag my ass into work.

"So you won't mind if I have drinks with Amy tonight, then?"

I stop in my tracks and turn back to look at Nico. He's sitting up in my bed, his hands clasped behind his head in a casual stance. Who the hell is Amy?

"Oh, we're just friends. We used to sleep together, but we're just friends now. She's a vitamin sales rep and we've been talking about adding a line of vitamins to my gym, but I usually keep our business talks in the gym. But maybe it would be better if we discussed our business over drinks instead."

Very nice. I feel like ripping Amy's head off, whoever the hell Amy is. But I get it. Point taken. "Fine, I'll do my best to keep my business with William in the office."

Nico thinks I'm walking back to him to give him a kiss. He's got such a damn, smug smile on his face. I pick up the pillow and hit him with it before heading to the shower. I hear him chuckling behind me as I stomp my way to the bathroom.

CHAPTER 43

Nico

I've never brought a woman to our monthly dinner. It's not that my mom and brothers would mind, I just never found one that I thought would still be around by the time the next month's dinner rolled around, so why bother introducing them? Elle baked cookies to bring, which is sweet, but I'm going to have to hide them from the kids to save them from possible food poisoning. She burned three batches before she finally got it right, or at least she thinks she did.

My niece Sarah takes Elle almost the minute we walk in and introduces her around like she's a shiny new toy. My mom seems curious and I catch her watching Elle a few times. She must like what she sees because she smiles to herself as she watches. I check on Elle every once in a while, but she doesn't look uncomfortable so I leave her to the women. She catches me looking at her each time, and smiles like a kid. It's hard for me to tear my eyes away.

"You got it bad, bro." Sam smiles at me before taking a swig from his beer bottle.

"Shut the fuck up."

Sam laughs. "What? It's about time. You had us worried you were going to get STDs the way you tore through women."

"I didn't tear through women."

"Yeah, ya did."

"You're just jealous, asshole."

"Jealous about what?" Elle's voice surprises me, I hadn't realized she was near me.

"Nothing." I snake my arm around her waist, pulling her close to me. "Come here." I kiss her forehead as I wrap my other hand around her waist. She looks up at me and smiles. Jesus Christ I'm so far gone for this woman that I do shit like kiss her forehead and smile just because she smiles. Yep, I'm god damn whipped. And I love every damn minute of it. It doesn't even bother me when I look up and find half my family watching us, smiling like complete idiots.

Sarah insists on sitting in between me and Elle during dinner. She's the only girl among the seven boys my brothers have spawned. She's wearing a silver princess crown, pink bodysuit, and her Girl Scout sash across her like Miss America. She's also wearing yellow rain boots and it's not raining. But whatever, she's freakin adorable and she seems to have taken a liking to Elle.

"Can I paint your nails after dinner?" I look over at Elle's manicured hands and try to save her, throw her a lifeline.

"I think Elle's nails are already painted, Sarah." Yeah, reasoning with her should work.

"I wasn't going to repaint them, Uncle Nico." She responds to me as she rolls her eyes, like I'm crazy for thinking she wanted to paint her nails, even though that's the exact question she asked. "I'm just going to polka dot them!"

Elle smiles at Sarah. "I'd love that...mine are too plain."

Sarah beams at Elle and looks back to me flatly, her face bearing the words "I told you so."

The pair chat their way through dinner, covering pressing issues such as favorite cookies, favorite color, favorite cartoon, and favorite fighter. There seems to be a running theme with Sarah's question topics. Elle pretends to struggle with her answer on the last question

183

and, for a second, I think things might go sour with Sarah, but instead she just jumps up and down, amused. "Elle, you're supposed to say Uncle Nico is your favorite fighter! I have a poster of him in my room and all. Uncle Nico gave it to me to scare away the monsters in my dreams, because he looks mean. Really mean." Sarah makes a face that is supposed to be mean, but it's freakin cute as hell instead. "And it works! Do you have monsters in your dreams? Uncle Nico, Elle needs a poster too!"

Everyone is laughing at Sarah's excitement, so they don't hear it when Elle leans in close and whispers to me, "I'll take a poster for over the bathtub. For next time."

The woman is going to be the death of me. Giving me a hard-on while sitting at a table surrounded by my family and next to a six-year-old.

"Go away with me this weekend?" We're driving back to Elle's, so I can't see her reaction to my question, but she doesn't keep me waiting long.

"Okay."

"Don't you even want to know where we're going?" Her answer is fucking awesome, but I'm curious.

"Nope. I don't care where we go, as long as I'm with you."

Yep, I love this fucking girl.

CHAPTER 44

Elle

"What about your training? Is there a gym?" We've been heading north for a long time, and I regret telling Nico I didn't want to know where we're going, because now curiosity has gotten the best of me. I keep asking him questions, trying to get a hint of our destination, but he doesn't budge an inch.

"There's no gym, but I'm planning on lots of cardio this weekend."

Nico smiles but keeps his eyes on the road as he drives in the dark. There aren't any street lights and the road has narrowed to one lane in each direction. I take in his handsome profile, the beautiful lines of his cheek leading to his square jaw. A jaw that hasn't seen a razor in twenty-four hours and the stubble makes him look even more rugged and handsome, if that's even possible.

"You're staring."

"I like what I'm looking at."

Nico takes his eyes off the road for a second and glances at me quickly and then they return to the road. But in that split second I see the green in his eyes and it makes me want him. His bright eyes light up his sexy, dark-tanned face. As he turns back to the road, he smiles and his stunning cheek dips, revealing the dimple that makes me weak in the knees. I don't know exactly what it is, but there is something about the contrast of how strong and masculine Nico is that mixes with his boyish, dimpled smile that does me in. I actually need to squeeze my legs shut to calm the swell growing between them. I have the urge to reach over and feel him. Start at his solid thigh and slowly follow the heat that will undoubtedly lead me to a place that will leave us both panting with need.

"We only have another five minutes drive, or I'd be pulling off to the side of the road the way you're looking at me."

I laugh at his comment, grateful that he can't see my face as it reddens. I've never been one to seek out physical contact with a partner. I usually enjoy it and participate in it actively, but I have just never been the pursuer. Yet with this man, I find myself unable to stop my body's natural reaction to being near him. It has a mind of its own when it comes to Nico Hunter.

We finally turn off the road and head down a long driveway, or perhaps it's a private street, I can't tell in the darkness. But we drive for a while and there are no longer any houses. There's a light off in the distance that seems to be in the direction of where we're going.

"Where are we?"

"Preach's lake house."

"I can't even tell there's a lake it's so dark."

"It's behind the house. Tomorrow in the daylight you'll be shocked you couldn't see it, the damn thing's huge."

We finally pull up to the house and I can see the light that was flickering in the distance is now on the porch. It's one of those solar lights that gives off a blue tint and barely enough brightness to see more than three feet ahead. But the porch looks huge, wrapping around the entire house. There's Adirondack chairs and small tables set up in various places that I can barely make out in the dark. Nico comes around and opens my door to help me down out of his SUV.

We make our way up the few stairs to the porch and Nico opens the front door with a key on his key ring. With the headlights now off, it's pitch dark except for the sole dim light sitting on the porch.

"Stay right here." Nico let's go of my hand and I can barely see what he's doing, just a slight change in the level of darkness shows me he's moving through the room. He doesn't bump into anything, so either the room is empty or he knows his way around well. A few seconds later, I hear the familiar sound of a match striking a flint and then a candle is lit on a small table up against a window.

"You're not going to turn on the lights and let me see the place? After keeping me in the dark about where we were going for hours?"

Nico laughs and I watch as he comes towards me, the one candle providing enough light for me to see him more clearly. "There's no electricity here."

"What do you mean there's no electricity?" My voice comes out almost appalled, because for a second I am.

"Preach calls it his sanctuary. No phone, no electricity, no cell service. No people for miles." Nico wraps his arms around my waist as he speaks and pulls me close against his body, making it easier to digest what he's telling me. Everything seems easy when I'm pressed up against the man. He makes me lose my wits, my edge, my common sense.

"You took me to a place with no electricity and no cell service." I have to try now to sound disturbed, because I'm not anymore. Not with his warm breath nuzzling its way onto my neck as he buries his head into my hair.

"I did." His sinful mouth finds its way to my ear, where his words are spoken quietly but they travel through me like heat through a coil and wake up every molecule in my body. The hair on the nape of my neck responds, prickling through a chill that breaks out all over my body in goose bumps.

"Come on, it's cool enough up here to make a fire." Nico releases me and my body is disappointed to lose contact so soon. He holds my hand and steers me through the dark house into a room at the back. After he's made a fire I can see the enormity of the fireplace. It's made of stone and I feel dwarfed by the sheer size of it.

"Wow, it's...incredible." The words don't do enough to describe it. The light from the fireplace casts a soft glow on the room and I can see that the walls of the room are all glass. It's too dark to see anything on the outside, but I imagine that I would be looking out at a lake if the sun was shining.

Nico is still standing by the fireplace, but now he's watching me as I take in the beauty of the room. "Jesus, Babe, you look like an angel standing there."

I smile at his compliment, I've never been good at accepting compliments, but with Nico, the way he speaks to me, I believe every word he says. I know I don't look like an angel, but to Nico, I do at this moment. Neither of us moves, both content in what the light finds for the other to see. Then his eyes find mine and everything else fades away...the darkness, the fireplace, the room, everything. None of it exists anymore. It's just us and everything seems so simple. It's one of those moments in life that you feel a shift. Like everything you've done before has lead to this point and whatever happens from this point on will be different. I don't know how or why, but I'm as certain of it as I've ever been of anything in my life. I'm in love with this man, and the realization doesn't even scare me. Not the slightest bit.

Nico walks to me slowly, his eyes never releasing mine. He stops as he reaches me, falling short of contact between our bodies, but just short. We're standing so close I have to tilt my neck back and look up at him to keep our eyes locked, but I don't dare move for fear that one of us will blink and the moment will be gone. He raises one of his big hands and softly brushes my hair back from my face, his touch is so tender and gentle. Slowly, he lowers his head down to mine and I think he's going to kiss me, his face is so close to mine that I can feel his breath on my lips, but he doesn't. He stops so we don't have to lose the contact of our locked eyes. And then everything I felt shift is confirmed and my world changes.

"I love you, Elle."

I don't have to think about my response. Because there's never been anything in my life I've been surer about. "I love you, too."

Then he kisses me. Sweetly. Gently. Passionately. Really kisses me...in a way that I've never been kissed before. It's not a prelude to sex or foreplay. It's love. Pure and simple, it's love pouring from both of us and connecting in a kiss. And in that moment I realize, I've never really been kissed before. I thought I'd been, but I wasn't. There was absolutely nothing before this kiss, and I can't wait to see what comes after.

By the time we break for air, I'm holding onto his shoulders in order to keep upright. Without his arms wrapped so tightly around me, I would be a puddle on the floor. My knees are weak and my arms are shaking and then there's the tears. The tears have welled up in my eyes and I can't stop them from falling when he looks at me that way. I'd heard people say they cried tears of happiness before, but I'd never given the term any thought. But that's what they are and they start falling. Streaming from my eyes as I smile up at the man that I'm madly in love with. And he with me.

He smiles back down at me and wipes the tears from my eyes. "You're smiling and crying."

"I know...I think fifteen years of holding back my emotions just got the best of me...and now you're in trouble." I laugh as I speak, realizing how ridiculous it must sound, but it's true. I haven't felt anything for fifteen years, really, and now I'm overwhelmed with emotions I hadn't even realized I was capable of anymore.

Nico smiles before he reaches down and lifts me into his arms, cradling me tightly against his chest. I wrap my arms around his neck. "What are you doing?"

"I'm taking the woman I love to bed to make love to her."

"Oh." His words are like music to my ears.

The next morning I wake to a familiar warm hand on my exposed back, rubbing gently up and down my spine. I turn my head to face the man I've professed my love to and he smiles at me. "Mornin."

"Morning." I smile back and can't help that it's a goofball smile, I feel satisfied and happy and completely and totally in love. I can't remember the last time I felt so relaxed. Telling Nico about my past has lifted a weight off my chest that I didn't even realize I was carrying.

Nico laughs at my smile. "I want to take you out onto the lake this morning before it gets too hot." He pushes my hair covering part of my face behind my shoulder and kisses my cheek.

"Okay."

"I could get used to this new agreeable woman that you've become." Nico lifts up and kisses my bare back, just above the sheet that is covering me from the waist down.

"And I could get used to waking up to this." He trails sweet gentle kisses up from the small of my back all the way to the nape of my neck.

"Come on, before we don't leave the bed all day." He abruptly stops kissing me and I miss the warmth of his body covering my back instantly.

I groan loudly, very unladylike, "Or we could just stay in bed all day?" I attempt to persuade him with an invitation.

"Not a chance. There's a dozen places I want to have you here."

"Have me?" Is he saying what I think he's saying?

Nico pulls back the sheet, exposing my naked ass, as I still lie face down on the bed. I've not yet made any attempt to move. He groans and smacks my ass playfully.

"I'm going to have you on the little island that's in the center of the lake. I can't wait to see you spread eagle in the middle of that patch of grass under the tree." I begin to sit up and I watch as Nico's light green eyes turn stormy. There's no hiding when he wants me and I love it. It's raw and real and he doesn't try to mask it for something it's not. Nico drinks me in and then takes a deep breath before his eyes return to mine. "And maybe even bent over the captains chair before we leave the dock if you don't hurry."

I expected the lake to be pretty, but nothing I could have imagined comes close to what I see when my eyes first take in the stunningly picturesque scenery right before me. Nico brings me a cup of coffee as I stare out the wall of glass where the darkness hindered my vision the night before, and wraps his thick arms around my middle as he stands behind me. "Beautiful right?"

"It's stunning. It doesn't even look real. It's all too perfect." I truly am in awe. It's not that I don't stop to appreciate nature, but the times that I do have become few and far between the last few years as I've thrown myself into my work and the city.

"I'm glad you like it." Nico squeezes me a little closer as he speaks.

"How could anyone not like it?" The trees are in bloom and the entire perimeter of the crystal clear sparkling lake is lined with tall purple and orange wildflowers. I wonder for a moment if they were planted, but then I think better of it and realize that nothing man-made could possibly be that beautiful.

Nico sighs, it's a sound of contentment. Happiness. I know because I feel the exact same way. "Do you come up here often?"

"I used to."

"Why did you stop?" Nico doesn't respond right away and it makes me think there is a story, something difficult that made him stop.

"I started coming here when I was fifteen. Preach used to bring me up to fish the lake. Sometimes my brothers would come, once in a while even my mom when she could get a full day off, which was rare."

I turn myself in Nico's arms...sensing the part of the story that made him stop coming was near. I look up at him and he continues with my full attention. "We had a good many parties up here after I won fights." His face is smiling as he recalls some of the good times. "Preach won't allow electricity, so my brothers and I used to fill the back of a pickup truck with coolers." He chuckles at the thought. "We could get a dozen coolers filled with beer in the back of a short cab."

I smile watching him, he has such nice family memories. Families coming together to celebrate their success around a lake filled with love and laughter. Something I longed for most of my younger years.

"So why did you stop coming?"

Nico's face drops and I almost wish I didn't ask, but I want to know everything about this man. What makes him happy or sad, smile or frown...all of it, the good and the bad. It's all part of what makes the man before me.

"Preach brought me up here after I tore apart my gym last year. After the fight." He doesn't need to explain which fight, it's just *the fight*. "It was ugly. I couldn't sleep without nightmares without the meds and I spent days trying to outrun the memories. It sucked. But Preach wouldn't leave me, no matter how many times I threatened his life and pushed him around."

I wait for him to continue, but nothing more comes. "And you haven't been back since?"

Nico shakes his head.

"So what made you bring me up here?"

He looks down at me and smiles. "I love this place. Some of my best memories are here." He kisses me chastely on the lips before continuing. "I've wanted to come back, chase away the haunted memories with new ones. Ones that will make me forget the bad ones."

God, the man is beautiful. And not just on the outside...on the inside too...and he doesn't even have to try. It's just who he is. Underneath 220 pounds of tattooed hard muscle that screams trouble is the most sensitive and beautiful soul I've ever met. For the first time since I was eight years old I feel like the luckiest girl on the planet.

The island in the center of the large lake is small, maybe the size of a house. But it's beautiful, with pristine sand, a small patch of grass, and a few simple weeping trees that look like they've been plucked off of a postcard that reads "Hello from Paradise." Sitting in the center of the lake emphasizes the enormity of its size... it's more than one hundred acres in size. Nico tells me that Preach saved for almost twenty years to buy the property and the lake. His father had owned a small piece of land and he'd loved the area since he was a kid. The reasons why are obvious.

"Let's go for a swim." Nico suggests.

"I don't have my bathing suit on." For a second I answer as if he might not realize I'm not wearing one. But then I see his smile. The dirty one that shows his deep creviced dimples and I'm sure he's had many women drop their panties without further effort.

"Don't need one."

"But what if someone sees."

"Do you think I'd let anyone get a glimpse of that fantastic ass that belongs to me, Babe?"

He has a good point. He's possessive and protective and there is no way there's a chance that anyone might see me naked if he's suggesting we swim without suits. I've spent fifteen years being conservative, it's time I lived a little. I don't respond with words. Instead, I stand from the blanket we're sitting on and take a step back, giving Nico a better view. He leans back, stretching out his long body, his elbows supporting him as he positions himself for my show with a lazy grin on his face. Slowly, I pull my t-shirt over my head, revealing a pink lace bra. Nico doesn't move, but his eyes rake over me with appreciation I can actually feel on my body. It's like a blanket of warmth and it covers me and fuels my nerve to keep on going.

I unbutton my shorts, slowly pulling the zipper down, allowing my thumb to reach up and graze the skin underneath the zipper that is still hidden. I'm not touching myself anywhere intimate, but it feels sexy and intimate just the same. With an exaggerated bend, I lean over and shake my hips suggestively, allowing my shorts to skim my legs and fall to the ground.

I stand, clad in only pink, lacy boy shorts and a matching demi cup bra and watch as Nico's eyes go dark. He begins to push up from his elbows, but I raise my pointer finger and motion no, I want to give him a show.

"Are you trying to kill me?" Nico's voice is husky, but he stays put as requested, even though I can see he's working to keep himself seated.

I reach behind me and undo my bra, slipping it off slowly before I speak. "No, I'm trying to give you new memories that will make you forget the bad ones."

Nico blows out a deep breath loudly and settles back on his elbows again. He's going to listen to me and let me do this for him. I stand before him in only my lacy panties and I'm not ready to take them off. I want to give him something to remember, something that will really sear into his brain and make him forget the last time he was here.

Reaching up, I slowly trace my breast with one hand, lazily allowing my fingernail to lightly scratch at my skin. I'm nervous, but I want to do this, so I close my eyes and try to surrender to the moment.

With my eyes still closed, I drag my fingernail over my swollen nipple and it swells even more under my touch. Slowly, I raise my finger to my mouth and suck, wetting my fingers before returning to my engorged nipple and coating it with my own silky fluids. It feels good, but I need more. Firmly, I grasp my own nipple between my thumb and forefinger and pinch. I feel it straight down to my toes and the sensitive skin between my legs tingles with anticipation. Another pinch, this time with more pressure and I feel wetness between my legs and I gasp at the sensation it sends through my body in a jolt.

I've touched myself before, but it never had such an effect on me. I need more, more friction, and I need it fast. My hand travels down my flat stomach and slips into the front of my panties. They're lace, so even though I'm still wearing them, there isn't much that Nico can't see.

"Fuck." Nico's gravelly voice vibrates through me, raising my arousal to a new high. I find my clit and gently rub it, making slow small circles. My head falls back and a low moan escapes my lips as I feel a familiar feeling build within me. And then he's on me. Touching and feeling and grabbing and biting, we go at it like wild animals. I'm not even sure when he undressed, but I'm insanely grateful that there aren't any clothes between us. I feel every ounce of his rock hard body, it feels so good that I think I may find my release before we even get started.

Nico growls as he takes my stiff nipple into his mouth and bites down hard. Pain, just shy of too much, shoots through me and my body begins to pulse on its own. He releases my aching nipple, but only enough to suck it back into his mouth and tease me. He swirls his tongue around, gently lathering it with attention, begging it to forgive him for the pain inflicted just moments ago.

He sucks his way from my breast up to my neck and eventually finds my mouth. His tongue leading mine in a dance that leaves me panting heavily when he turns his attention to my ear. "I need inside of that pussy you made so wet for me."

His words set off a moan that comes from deep within me and I feel my body begin to contract. I need him inside of me too. Now. So badly. "Please." I don't even care that it comes out as begging. I have no shame when it comes to the pleasures of this man.

He lifts me up into his arms before dropping down on one knee, gently positioning me on the grass. Two seconds ago we were biting and grabbing and now he is so gentle with me. He takes care of me first, makes sure I am okay, putting his own desire on the back burner to tend to me. It's one of the things that I love about him, something that's hard to put into words and explain to your girlfriend when you're on a rant to explain why you've fallen in love with a man. He just puts me first. Always.

I expect to feel his warm body on top of mine, but it's not, so I open my eyes to see what's taking him so long and find him looking down at me. What I see takes my breath away. I try to speak, but I have no words. He's mentally searing the moment into his brain, capturing it forever like an artist with a brush. I can feel it. It's adoration and lust and love and every other heartfelt emotion rolled up into one perfect man who loves me and couldn't hide it if he tried.

Unable to speak, I'm so filled with emotions that I can only reach up and offer him my hand. He takes it without a word and gently steadies himself on top of me, propping himself up on his arms, his muscular forearms on either side of my face. "I love you." I finally find the words for the perfect moment he's given me.

His head comes down and he kisses me as I feel his thick head push into me. I deepen the kiss as it smothers my whimpers as his thick cock fills me. I know we should go slower, but I can't wait any longer. It's a tight fit normally, but without the slow ease in that Nico usually controls, it's snugger than usual. But it feels so good, so right. I'll worry about being sore tomorrow.

With the base of his hard length pushed up against me, Nico steadies himself. He wants to give me time to adjust, but I'm not waiting anymore. I buck up the little that I can move underneath his weight, tilting my pelvis ever so slightly, but it allows him to sink even deeper. A gasp slips from deep within me.

"Fuck, Babe. Are you okay?"

"I will be if you would stop treating me like glass and get that tight ass of yours going." I dig my nails into his ass to accentuate my need.

Nico's eyebrows raise in surprise, but I'm going to get my way one way or the other. I reclaim his mouth and bite down hard on his bottom lip, so hard I'm surprised I don't taste blood. But it gets his attention and it's the attention that I want. He pulls almost all the way out and then slams back into me...hard. I moan. It's exactly what I need.

And then he does it again, this time swiveling his hips on a forceful draw down and he hits that sensitive place on the inside. I tremble as my body begins to convulse around him. But he keeps on going, pumping in and out, in and out, each time rubbing me within an inch of my orgasm until we are both within seconds of climax. Nico reaches between us and strokes my pulsating clit with his wide thumb and it's enough to push me over the edge. I moan his name as my body begins to climax, pulsating wildly as wave after wave of bliss rolls over me. I feel the heat of Nico's release pour into me and I think I'm about to hit bottom, but I keep falling, his release prolonging my own.

By the time we leave the next evening, there is no doubt in my mind that we've replaced Nico's memories with new ones that he won't soon forget.

CHAPTER 45

Elle

The last few weeks have been, without a doubt, the happiest weeks of my life. I've found a balance between my work and my time with Nico, and Lawrence actually seems happy that I'm working fewer hours these days. His own health issues have been a soft reminder of life's priorities and it seems to have spilled over into how he is managing the office. The timing couldn't be more perfect.

I still think about my past, but I haven't had another nightmare since I told Nico. It's odd, sometimes it feels like I've lightened what I carry around with me, but only because Nico is sharing the weight. We talk about it openly now and it seems to help. Each day it gets a little bit easier.

I can't remember the last time I saw the delivery man for dinner. Nico's in training for his big fight and he seems to love to feed me. We alternate between our apartments, but we've slept in the same bed almost every night since we came back from Preach's house on the lake. I thought we had hit a high note, and things would have nowhere to go from there, but I'm finding I like the day to day ordinary with Nico almost as much as the special times. I'm in a domestic bliss of sorts, a place I never thought I'd find. A place that just didn't seem in the cards for me. But here I am…and I couldn't be happier.

I leave work a little early, it's an important day for Nico. He finally finds out who he'll be fighting in the championship fight. Not that the name will mean anything to me, but I want to be there for him.

I hit traffic on the way to the gym and barely make it there before the live announcement that is going to be made on T.V. The gym is full, but it's not humming with its usual bevy of men hitting things or lifting poundage that exceeds my body weight. Instead, they're all gathered around the T.V. that hangs from the corner of the cardio area. The sound is loud and the scene is upbeat and jovial. As always, Nico clocks me the minute that I walk in. He's talking to an up-and-coming young fighter I've seen around before, but he watches every step I take. I wonder if the poor guy even notices he's lost Nico's attention.

"Love the suit." Nico wraps his arm around my waist possessively the second I approach. I wore his favorite red suit, knowing I would be leaving the office early to go straight to see him. The hem is a little shorter than most of my others, but I barely made it out of it the last time I wore it, so I thought he might have taken a liking to it. I was right. I love that Nico finds me sexy in a suit. Some men would be intimidated by a woman dressed for business, but not Nico. Instead of intimidated, he finds it arousing.

The newscasters come on and we join the others around the T.V. The announcer talks for a little while about Nico's career, footage plays on the screen from *the fight*. Nico's grip on my waist tightens as they discuss the death of his former opponent, I'm only grateful that they didn't decide to replay the blow that ended the fight.

Finally, the President of the MMA Fighting Association comes on the screen and reminds everyone that one week from today the championship fight will take place. He then makes a big to-do about opening an envelope that contains the name of the challenger, as if he didn't already know, and the name is announced. Trevor Crispino. The room falls silent. Apparently I'm the only one that the name means nothing to. I scan the room for some indication of why Mr. Crispino's name is met with such empathy, but everyone seems shell-shocked.

Especially Preach. I vaguely remember Nico telling me he thought it would be a fighter named Caputo.

Nico disappears before I can ask him what is going on and suddenly the quiet room erupts in chatter. There's lots of "no fuckin way" comments and a few "this is bullshit, he's not even a contender" remarks, but I'm still lost. I make my way through to Preach, who's still staring at the floor. His reaction is making me feel even more panicked.

"Preach, what's wrong with Trevor Crispino?" I ask hesitantly, not really sure I want to hear the answer, because I know it's bad. Really bad.

Preach looks up at me, his eyes are glassy and he looks sad. My heart lurches into my stomach. "He's Frankie's brother. The boy that died in the *the fight*. They're trying to make it a grudge match. But the kid shouldn't even be in the ring with the likes of Nico. He's no match. Nico will kill 'em."

I'm sure the last words weren't meant literally, but sometimes things that aren't meant to come out that way, come out the way they should be spoken in the end, anyway.

I find Nico in his loft, sitting in the dark. His elbows on his knees, head dropped low in his hands. I wait for a minute before I approach, wondering if he will acknowledge I've entered the room. The gate on the elevator door is loud, there's no way he didn't hear me come in. But he just sits there quietly, even as I make my way to him and rest my hand on his shoulders, he doesn't move.

"You okay?" My voice is low, but the room is so quiet, there is no mistaking that he can hear me. Yet he doesn't answer.

I bend down to eye level with him in the darkness. It doesn't matter that he can't see me, I'll be harder to ignore when I'm so close.

"What can we do?"

Nico lets out a heavy rush of air before he wraps his big hand around my neck, leaning his forehead against mine. "Just let me hold you."

That I can do. I only wish I had more to offer to comfort him. His voice sounds raw and pained. I can only imagine what he must be feeling. If my own crushed heart and knotted stomach are any indication, then his own pain must be unbearable. How can they do this to him? Put him in the cage with the brother of the man he killed? A man that is no match for his power. Aren't there rules or something?

My initial shock and sadness is starting to wear off and I've moved onto pissed. Mad, angry, ready to take on a fight of my own. "We'll get you out of this. You don't have to do this. This isn't sportsmanship, this is for ticket sales." Have they no conscience? And what about safety? Preach said the brother is no match, that Nico will kill him. Aren't they supposed to match up ability? I hear my own breath speed up, my anger getting the best of me.

Nico chuckles quietly. It's barely there and I'm not even sure if what I heard is the sound of his laughter. But then he speaks and I know that I'm not mistaken, "Might have to keep you home for the fight...afraid you're gonna jump in the cage and beat the crap out of the guy for me." I can hear the smile in his voice as he speaks.

"I might." His smile is returned, even if he can't see it.

I spend the next three days researching, analyzing, and generally looking for any possible loophole to get him out of the fight. I've called in every favor I had and sought opinions from each and every lawyer that might remotely be able to help us. Even William. But we all come up with the same conclusion, the contract is airtight. Of course, Nico can walk away from the fight and pay the penalty clause. But he won't do that. Preach's finances are on the line too. I don't know why I didn't see the motive behind making Preach invested in the fight, but I didn't.

Whoever drew up the terms of the contract new exactly what they were doing. They knew Preach and Nico well, but not just the fighter and trainer.

They've exploited the relationship between these two men on a personal level, knowing Preach would never let Nico pay his penalty and Nico would never let Preach take such a financially draining hit. Two stubborn men that will protect each other until the end, no matter what the cost to themselves.

And it's gotten even worse. Preach has decided that the fight will be good for Nico, that he needs to move on and getting through this disaster of a fight will help him push through the remnants of emotional ties that remain. He's even started to get Nico to believe some of his bullshit. That a grudge match is some sort of sick redemption...a shot at salvation.

I jump when I hear the front door to the office open. It's after ten and I promised Regina I'd lock it behind her when she left hours ago, but I was so engrossed in what I was searching for, that I completely forgot. But then I feel it, the unmistakable presence of the man that makes my heart rate speed up. I'm absolutely certain that if I was hooked up to an EKG machine, it would be able to record each step closer that Nico Hunter takes in my direction.

"The door isn't locked." Nico's voice is tense. He's protective, and my lack of concern for my own safety is something I've learned he isn't fond of.

"I must have forgotten." I look up, offering the lame excuse. I watch as Nico takes in the mess that was once my office. I have piles of papers and journals strewn all over the office and my garbage overflows with crumpled yellow legal paper where I've started to map out an angle to break the contract, but didn't work in the end.

"Big case?" His eyes gloss over my desk to accentuate what he is referring to.

"Sort of." I'm not lying...at the moment it's the most important case I have. And the reality is that it's the only case I've worked on in three days. All my other work can wait.

Nico pushes off the door frame where he rests and walks to my desk, taking a piece of paper off it, and reading a few lines before putting it back down. He takes a pile of clipped documents from the other side of the desk and does the same thing, reading a little to get a feel for what I've been working on. He knows what I'm doing, this act is for my benefit.

"Come on, we're going home." He's standing on the other side of my desk. As much as I love hearing Nico tell me we're going *home,* I'm not ready yet. I need a little more time to work my way through my latest strategy. There has to be a way to get him out of the damn contract.

"I'm not done yet."

I don't miss Nico's jaw clenching, it's ridiculously sexy. A deep line on his chiseled cheek forms and his eyes turn a deep greenish grey. He looks strong and menacing and I would bet most would take a step back with the scary vibe that he throws off. But not me, I hold my ground and stay put, albeit a little more aroused than I was a minute ago. We stare at each other, each waiting for the other to back down, and I wonder if we're going to be here a while. But then Nico breaks the standoff.

He doesn't release my eyes as he stalks around my desk and pulls back my chair, leaning his big frame down to reach my eye level. His thick frame blocks me into my seat, one hand on each arm of my chair. "You need to do anything before I take you out of here?"

"I…I…" I was going to say that I'm almost done and just need a few minutes, but I don't have the chance to finish my thought. I'm lifted out of my chair and tossed over Nico's shoulder in one fluid movement. The barbaric move should piss me off, but instead it makes me smile. I'm happy that my head is tossed over his back, so he can't see that I'm actually enjoying myself. Challenging this man has somehow become foreplay to me.

He doesn't release me until I'm in the passenger seat of his car. He buckles me in while I sit with my arms crossed over my chest, feigning anger. After he tugs on the belt, double checking I'm secure, he kisses me chastely on the lips before jogging around to his side of the car.

"What about my car?" I throw a little extra attitude in with my question.

"I'll drive you to work in the morning."

I let out an exaggerated sigh. "You're bossy."

"You're stubborn." My mouth drops open at his comment, even though I know it's true. But Nico just finds my response amusing and chuckles.

CHAPTER 46

Nico

Usually the night before a fight I have dinner with Preach and get a pep talk. But I pass on the tradition and Elle stays at my place instead. I finally convinced the stubborn woman to stop her fifteen hour a day quest to break my contract. At least I'd like to think I convinced her, but it might also be because we ran out of time, considering the fight is tomorrow. The woman is a challenge when she sets that damn smart mind on something, to say the least.

Elle doesn't agree, but Preach thinks the fight will be good for me. We studied Trevor's last few fights. The kid has improved. A lot. He's not the same stupid, cocky fighter that he was a year ago. He's matured, found patience. The fight isn't as lopsided as we all originally thought, although I'd be fooling myself if I pretended that what happened with his brother didn't factor into the League's decision on who to match up for the championship fight. My fights are always profitable for the League, a sellout. But I can't remember the last time MMA got as much press as it did this week. My face has been plastered on mainstream news, not just the channels dedicated to sports.

I lift her onto the island counter as I make dinner. She's still wearing her work clothes and I'm definitely not prompting her to change. I like her in the smart looking crap she wears. It's a turn-on, almost like fucking the hot librarian, only better because it's Elle.

Some guys won't have sex before a fight, they think the pent up frustration gives them an edge. Me, I prefer not to fight with blue balls. I've never been one to look for an angle. I study my competitor. I work my ass off training. I fight hard. I'm good. It's as simple as that. Plus, looking at Elle swinging those long damn legs propped up on my kitchen counter, there's not much of a chance where things are going to go later. I look at her and she smiles. It's that damn goofy grin. It may be sooner, rather than later.

After we finish dinner, I can see something is on Elle's mind. I've said it before, but for a lawyer, she's pretty easy to read. And a crap liar. "What's going on, Babe?"

Her eyebrows pull together and shift down, her face telling me she isn't even aware that she's showing her hand. "Nothing…what do you mean?"

"Something's bothering you."

Her face relaxes a little, but there's still tension underneath her forced smile. "No…I'm fine."

"Shit liar, Babe. I told you that."

She smiles. "Maybe I'm just a little nervous." She holds up her two fingers, measuring a small space between them to indicate she's just a tiny bit nervous. Her fingers may say a little, but her face screams much more.

Elle goes to sit next to me on the couch, but I grab her arm and pull her down on to my lap instead. "What are you nervous about?"

She rings her hands together, looking down, avoiding my eyes. I lift her chin, forcing her eyes to mine and repeat myself. "What are you nervous about?"

"The fight."

"Okay." I brush the hair away from her face, she looks worried, almost vulnerable. "I'm not going to get hurt, I can take this guy, Babe."

Nervously, she bites her bottom lip. I'm off base. There's more to the worry resonating from her. "I know. I mean, I'll always worry about you getting hurt. I can't help that. But..." She hesitates, considers her words.

"What then?"

"I know you and Preach think winning this fight will help you get past things, but I'm worried that it will bring it all back. I've seen him. He looks like his brother."

She's right, he does. He looks just like Frankie. It's like some sort of twisted fate fucking with me. And I've worried about the same thing. But I can't allow that to control me anymore. I push it to the back of my mind and keep it there each time it finds its way to the surface. It's all about control. Martial arts is as much about the mind as it is the body. Both must endure, submit to complete control. Work together.

"Preach thinks winning the fight will help me get past things. But I already know what it takes. And you've brought me further along in the last two months than a year and a half of trying to work it out on my own ever did. Before I met you, I was hitting my head against a concrete wall, going nowhere fast. Only I didn't know it. Didn't even realize I was stuck, until I met you and took that first step." Elle gives me a hesitant smile. Some of the worry disappears from her face... but not all of it. So I go for broke, being the fucking sap this incredible woman has made me into.

"When we met, we were two injured souls. Both keeping the real out of our lives for fear of what we might find. But nothing could have kept us apart. I never believed in destiny. Thought that was a bunch of crap for people who read too many books. Until I met you. You're it for me, Babe. I didn't even know I was missing something until I found you, but now I don't know how I got through a day without what you've given me. You're my soul mate. As sappy as it sounds, it's god damn true. Nothing has ever been truer in my life. So no, I'm not worried about this fight not helping me heal from my past, because it's you who does that for me. You've filled all the cracks in my heart and made me better. I never thought I'd say this after what I went through, but I'm the luckiest bastard on this earth."

She cries. That's how she responds to my gut wrenching, pussy-whipped declaration that we're soul mates. Tears stream down her face and, even though she's smiling through the tears, I want to make the tears go away.

CHAPTER 47

Elle

I never thought I'd be happy. I was content with flatlining my way through life. It was good enough. Keeping out the highs and the lows was my favorite past time. No emotions meant nothing ever got out of control, and keeping control was higher on my priority list than breathing. Until I met him. He makes my heart race and my breathing hitch, and that's just when he walks in the room. Don't even get me started on what that face does to me. Or those hands…especially when they're moving all over my body like he can't get enough of me. I can feel his need for me in his touch. But his words, that's what does me in. They're raw and honest and filled with emotions, and I can actually feel my heart swell as they're spoken.

He wipes away my tears with concern on his face. I'm sure he thinks I've lost my mind as I smile through my crying after listening to the most beautiful thing anyone has ever said to me. I'm the one whose head is usually filled with words. But right now I find myself at a loss for something beautiful to say in return. So I say what I feel and hope it's enough. "I love you."

He smiles, the worry leaving his face. "Love you too, Babe."

And then I kiss him, the tears still falling, my mouth still smiling, and a sob escapes me as our tongues find each other. I'm a mess, but it's beautiful and real and I can't get enough of him. Not now, not ever.

He's right. We're two lost souls that found each other and became one. And I'm the luckiest girl on the planet.

There's still hours before the fight, but I'm ready to go right now. It's a sold out championship fight, but Nico gave me four tickets of my own. My stepbrother, of course, has texted me half a dozen times to make sure we're still on for the day. It's a close race who is more exited, Max or Vinny. Both probably didn't sleep last night with anticipation pulsing through their veins.

I'm excited I also got to invite Regina and Lawrence. Regina because, well, she's the best friend I have ever had...and I think she's more excited about my relationship with Nico than I am, at times, if that's even possible. After all these years, she couldn't wait to see me throw myself back into the land of the living. And Lawrence, he's more than my boss, he's been like a dad to me the last few years. Plus, it's the first bit of excitement his wife has let him have since his heart surgery. She's afraid too much might give him a heart attack.

At first I've forgotten what I'm wearing when Nico catches sight of me, he hasn't seen the t-shirt Vinny made for me. I'm not sure if the kid did it on purpose, but it's tight, very tight, hugging all my curves. My shirt is different than the one Vinny wore last time. It's a full body shot with Nico facing forward. He looks more like a model than a fighter.

Nico freezes in place for a minute, gracing me with a devilish smile. "I like your shirt."

I feel my face heat and I know I'm turning a nice shade of pink. "It's my new favorite shirt. I can keep you pressed up against me all day, even in public." I respond coyly.

Nico stalks to me. "I'll press the real thing up against you all day in public, Babe. You don't have to ask twice." He's smiling like he's kidding, but I know he's serious. He wraps his arms around my waist and pulls me tight against his warm, hard body. He's wearing only a pair of running shorts and my body responds to his rough touch, even though it's been only hours since I've had him inside of me.

I'm flustered. "Don't you have a fight to get ready for?" My voice comes out throatier than I had intended, but I just can't help myself around him.

Nico presses into me, I can feel his throbbing erection pushing against my stomach. "They can't start the fight without me." He grabs half my ass in one of his massive hands and squeezes hard. His head lowers with intention to take my mouth, but the buzzer downstairs rings.

"Ignore it." I feel the words on my lips as he devours my mouth. My body gives in almost immediately and a small moan escapes my lips as he lifts me underneath the knees and cradles me in his arms as he heads toward the bed.

The buzzer rings again and neither of us break the kiss, even though I'm certain he hears it too. But then it buzzes again, this time more insistently. Whoever is downstairs waiting to come up isn't going away. Nico growls loudly, as he sets me down and stands. "Don't move, I'll get rid of whoever it is." A stream of expletives leave his mouth as he makes his way to the poor fool who is about to feel his wrath.

I lie in the bed for a moment, my breath slowly returning to almost normal as I wait for Nico's return. But then I hear voices and I realize that whoever it is has no fear of the irrational man that went in a frenzy to get rid of them.

I fix myself as best I can and head to the living room to see who's arrived. My hair is fingered back in place and my shirt is readjusted, but there isn't anything I can do with the heat on my face.

"Ma, you didn't need to bring Vinny by the house. I wouldn't have forgotten to pick him up. *And I told him that twenty times in the last twenty four hours.*" Nico catches me in the doorway and gives me a look like he may injure someone before the fight, but for some reason I only find it funny. He's cute when he's frustrated.

"Hi Mrs. Hunter. Hi Vinny." I smile and the two step around Nico who was blocking their passage for entry. Nico looks at me like I've just welcomed the devil into his home, instead of two of his biggest fans.

"You're wearing the t-shirt!" Vinny is excited and smiling.

"Of course I am. It's the coolest t-shirt I own." I wink at him and the all-confident boy turns shy for half a second before turning to face Nico.

"You like it Nico?" It's sweet how the boy wants Nico's approval, I just hope Nico doesn't flatten his enthusiasm because they interrupted a private moment.

Nico looks at me and takes my shirt in again, as if he is seeing it for the first time. His eyes go hooded and no response is really needed. The kid smiles as he watches Nico, knowing Nico couldn't be happier.

"Yeah kid. It's perfect." He takes a deep breath and exhales.

All of Nico's brothers and their wives are already seated when Vinny, Max, and I finally find our seats. Between my friends and his family, we fill almost two rows. My stepfather managed to pick up the security job for the fight, and it makes me feel bad that I can't invite mom too. I've told her about Nico, but even that made her nervous. There is no way she would be able to handle a live fight. Too many bad memories.

My stepfather spends a few minutes at our row and I get to introduce him to Nico's family. It's an odd feeling blending our families together, but when I take a minute to look around, I realize everyone feels right at home. My stepfather is chatting away and laughing with Nico's mom and oldest brother, and Vinny and Max are in their own little world. It brings a warm feeling to take it all in…I haven't felt like I had a family in so long. It's not my mom's fault, I just wouldn't let anyone in. I didn't even realize it until Nico snuck into my heart and opened it wide for others.

The announcer steps into the cage and my body goes tense. It's really going to happen now. I've pretended that it wasn't, that I had time before I had to go through watching Nico do this. But there's no more time left. What if he freezes again, only this time he gets hurt? Or if he hurts the brother? Will he be able to live with himself after what happened last time? I suddenly feel sick to my stomach.

"Elle?" I hear Regina speak, but I can't respond. I'm frozen in place, staring at the announcer like I'm waiting for something to happen any second. "Elle!" Regina grabs my arms and snaps me out of my trance. "Are you okay? You're white as a ghost."

I nod my head, but she isn't buying it. She knows me too well. "Come on, let's get out of here. This is too much." My arm is in her hand and she's already starting to pull me in her direction.

"No!" My voice comes out louder than I anticipated and I'm suddenly grateful for the announcer who just sent my mind into a tailspin. He's drowning me out with his loud words fired off in rapid succession, but their meaning doesn't register with me. I force myself to look at Regina so she knows I'm okay. "I can't leave. I need to be here."

Regina searches my eyes like she's looking for something. She still looks nervous, but she stops tugging at my arm. "Okay, okay. Let's sit then. Drink some water. Please."

I take the water to make Regina happy and try to focus on what the announcer is rattling on about.

"Ladies and Gentlemen, the moment you have all been waiting for. The match to end all matches, more than a year and a half in the making. The man, the myth, the legend, ladies need no introduction, the one, the only Nico 'The Laaaaaady Killlllller' Hunter."

The crowd goes insane. Vinny and Max are standing on the top of their seats jumping up and down so hard that I think they might break the chairs. Nico's mom, who is normally subdued, is screaming with hands on either side of her mouth. And his brothers are high fiving, fist pounding, and jumping up to smash each other with their own chests. The moment of insanity does wonders for my nerves, I can't help but smile at our crazy gang.

I'm impatiently waiting for Nico to enter the room, but I don't have to turn to know the minute he steps into the arena. The hairs on the back of my neck stand up and the room that I didn't think could get much louder ratchets up ten decibels. The sound is almost deafening. I turn to watch him make his way down the aisle, but it's difficult to see him behind the dozen bleach blonde women in bikinis and high heels who are marching down the aisle in front of him. Each carries a sign over their head bearing various testaments of love to "The Lady Killer."

I try in vain to see his face as he passes, but I'm too short for his sizeable entourage. It's not until he steps in the cage do I get a clear shot of his face. One of the brazen, scantily clad bikini girls makes a big commotion bending over in exaggerated form and kissing him on the cheek. It's only his side profile, but I catch his jaw clench and I smile to myself knowing the kiss was a setup and clearly unwelcome. And then he turns, and his eyes land directly on me. There is no search through the crowd, our eyes just find each other, like metal to a magnet, inexplicably pulled to each other without effort. He just needs to see I'm really here, but it's just reinforcement, he knew I was here the minute he walked in the room.

After a few minutes, the crowd finally dies down enough for the announcer to speak over them, although they're still going pretty strong.

"Ladies and Gentlemen, in the blue corner tonight, we have a man set for revenge. He's been waiting eighteen months for his chance to take back his family's honor...I give you, Trevor 'The Aaaaaaaa-vennnnnnnnnn-ger' Crispino."

Unlike last time, the crowd doesn't boo. Even Nico's family falls silent. There are some cheers from his fans, but most say nothing and I don't know if it's out of respect for Nico, his contender, or his late brother. Either way it sends a chill up my spine at the mere mention of the horror that was his brother's last fight.

After a few more mind-numbing announcements, the two men are sent to their respective corners. It's funny how my reason for worry changes, yet the worry stays the same. The last time I sat in this room I was worried that watching men come to blows would be a trigger for me. Something that would dredge up the memories of the past that I'd worked so hard to tuck away. But as I sit here today, I'm still worried about Nico's fight, yet it no longer has anything to do with my own self-preservation. All of my worry is for the man in the ring, how he'll manage to handle striking a face that is all too familiar. The similarities are haunting and it isn't even my nightmare. I worry that he'll freeze and get hurt, or that he won't and the emotional damage will take its toll later. Either way, it's hard to see a win for Nico at the end of this fight, no matter who comes out the victor.

I hold my breath as the fight begins and the two men meet in the middle. I want to look away, save myself the pain of watching it all unravel before my eyes, but I can't seem to allow myself to blink for fear of missing even a second. Nico strikes first, not giving his opponent time to even acclimate before knocking him back three steps with a thundering hit to the left side of his jaw.

As much as I struggle seeing the two men fighting to win something back, something that was taken wrongly from both of them, there is a sense of relief that Nico seems to be back to fighting the way that made him a champion. But my relief is short lived. Not ten seconds after I finally exhale, letting out the breath I had been holding, Trevor lands a kick to Nico's chest and Nico stumbles, his back hitting hard against the unyielding cage. His back arches with the contact, and I see his face register pain, but he quickly recovers. Sitting so close, I can see the toll each blow takes on their faces.

By the end of the first round, both men have taken and delivered harsh blows dealt with brute force strength. I don't claim to have any experience judging a match, but, to me, Nico is the clear leader as they take their seats in their respective corners. His blows are stronger, more precise. And he has the ability to recover faster from the ones he receives. But all in all, it doesn't appear to be an unfair fight.

Again in round two it's Nico who comes out blazing. He strikes fast and furious and lands a series of kicks which almost knocks Trevor to the ground, but his opponent somehow remains on his feet. Trevor regains his footing and takes aim at Nico, with a windup and punch that Nico manages to avoid by weaving, leaving Trevor plunging forward with the sheer momentum of the hit that never lands. Nico sees an opportunity and seizes it, pounding brutally on the man's back before he has time to recover from his missed punch. It's all too much, too fast, and Trevor falls forward, landing first on his knees, before both arms go wide and he plummets face first into the mat below. For no more than a split second, he lays still on the ground. But that's all it takes. I watch as something passes over Nico's face and everything changes.

Nico just stands there, blankly staring at his opponent, even as Trevor recovers, taking his time to get up, wobbling to his feet before regaining his footing. It's as if he's quit the fight, except there's still more than two minutes on the clock until the end of the round. But even though Nico might have thrown in the towel, his opponent sees it as an opportunity. He hits Nico with a left, then a quick right. The second punch landing so hard that I watch in slow motion as Nico's head swings to the side and blood splatters from his nose all over the shiny grey canvas below.

I'm watching in horror as Nico is pummeled, each series of blows taking my breath away. He's not even protecting himself, he's just standing there and taking it, like it's his punishment and he needs to be man enough to accept it. Preach is screaming like a madman from the sideline, trying to snap Nico out of it, but it's as if he doesn't even hear him. I wince at each strike, silently begging for the ref to stop the fight. I don't know the rules, but this can't be legal. Clearly, the ref sees that Nico has checked out and being in the cage is dangerous to a man that won't even protect himself. But they let the fight go on and on, and it's the longest two minutes of my entire life.

By the time the bell sounds at the end of the round, Nico is a bloody mess and I want to die. I feel helpless and I want to run into the cage and grab him and hold him tight against me and tell him everything is going to be okay. Only I can't.

The crowd doesn't know what to make of things either. The once frenzied chant of *Nico! Nico!* has died out and even Vinny and Max are eerily silent in their seats. It's as if they've all accepted the path that Nico has chosen...but I can't. I won't. I refuse.

The final round starts off almost the same as the last one ended, with Nico getting his face pummeled and him doing little to change things. I don't understand why everyone is so quiet. His brothers are all sitting and his mother sits silently on the edge of her chair, looking pale, her face turned away from the fight. She can't even bear to watch.

I just can't sit and quietly watch him go down without a fight. So I don't. I get up on my chair and start screaming. Like a loon. The people around me are staring, but I don't care. Screw them, they were all chanting his name when he was winning, but where are they now? After a few more punches that few men would be able to endure, let alone stand after, Trevor lunges and takes Nico down to the mat. The two men wrestle around for a few seconds, and then Trevor emerges on top, Nico's arm pinned behind his back, his head to the ground.

"Get up Nico! God damn it, Get up!" My screams are torn from my lungs, each word burning as it bleeds from me. I don't know if he hears me yelling, but somehow I doubt it since Preach is closer and can't seem to get his attention. But then something happens. Nico lifts his head from the mat, his arm still pinned behind his back, and I could swear, for just a split second, he looks right at me.

There's less than a minute left in the match, but we both know that so much can change in a single minute. The course of an entire life can be redirected, a man can choose to live, a man can die unexpectedly. Nothing is over until you call it quits or you take your last breath.

I have no idea how Nico gets himself out of the hold that Trevor had him in without breaking his own arm, but less than two seconds have ticked from the clock and Nico is back on his feet and there's a fire in his eyes. Trevor gets back up and readies himself, expecting to continue the fight, but it's no longer a continuation, it's suddenly a whole new fight. Nico lands a blow to the ribs and his opponent staggers back three steps. There's no time for Trevor to recover, to regain his footing, before Nico lunges, taking him down to the mat. And then Nico's on top, landing blow after blow, each more heartbreaking than the next, even though it's Nico I want to come out unscathed.

There's less than ten seconds on the clock when Nico backs off slightly, but his stubborn opponent lifts his head, trying desperately to get back on his weary feet. And then Nico winds up and strikes. Hard. The man's head wobbles, seemingly unhinged from side to side, his eyes rolling back into his head before they both close. I watch in slow motion as his head bounces up and down twice more before finally coming to rest lifelessly on the mat.

The arena goes silent. There are twenty thousand people in one room, yet I can hear the paramedic who rushed into the cage bark out orders and the ref instructs the men in suits watching from the sidelines that he's calling the fight. KO.

They wave something under the unconscious fighter's nose and I see his head shake from side to side. He's awake and alive and there's a collective sigh heard around the arena. After a few minutes, Trevor gets up with assistance from his trainer and walks out of the cage. But Nico is still standing there, staring at the place where Trevor once laid, even as the ref raises his arm in victory. The crowd goes wild, but I see it in Nico's face, there's no cause for celebration.

The whole way down to find Nico, I fret he may chase me away when I arrive at the locker room. I'm surprised to find a dozen people waiting in line outside his door. Even more surprised to find as many already inside. Photographers vie for photos of the new champion, but I can see he's in no mood. Two of the bikini bimbo's from the entrance parade are trying to snuggle up on either side of him as pictures are snapped excitedly. I know it's all part of marketing, but my nerves are shot and I have no patience left.

"Don't touch him." I warn as one of them goes to lift her leg and wrap it around Nico's side. She stops and looks me up and down, smirking at my t-shirt, she probably thinks I'm some lonesome groupie, hoping to get lucky tonight. That I'm no match for her open invitation to a sure thing. But I have no time or patience to pretend I care what she thinks. Nico watches me closely as I take the few steps to close the distance between us.

"Let's get out of here." I'm relieved at Nico's words. If he hadn't suggested leaving, I probably would have demanded it.

There are too many people to count yelling at Nico that he can't leave when we walk out the door. But neither one of us cares.

CHAPTER 48

Elle

It's been almost two days now. Nico hasn't pushed me away like last time, but he may as well have, because he's closed me out all the same…along with everyone else. I've tried everything…just holding him, quietly talking, even cuddling up to him bare ass, still I get no response. I'm starting to think Preach is right, he needs a doctor.

It broke my heart the first night when he stared blankly at the ceiling. He didn't say it, but I knew why he couldn't close his eyes. I went through the same thing for years. Instead of seeing black and calm, allowing yourself to drift into dreamland, you see that moment, the one frozen in time in your head. And then you're afraid to close your eyes. Afraid to sleep, afraid of the nightmares that you know will come. Terrified to be forced to relive it all again in your head, because it will all seem so real.

Yesterday I finally took the pills that Preach had been trying to give me to push on him since the first night. His body needs to rest, the physical injuries demand time to heal. Nico may have been the victor, but his body took a relentless beating in those short minutes that he surrendered. He's swollen and cut and black and blue. Everywhere. I held ice to his injuries when he finally slept, rotating different places on his body every fifteen minutes for more than ten hours, until there was nothing cold left in the freezer to hold against him. Those pills work, he didn't once move…not from the ice held against him or from my touch.

But today it's gotten worse. A sick, twisted part of me almost wishes that he was still drugged and sleeping. At least then I could pretend that everything was normal and he was just recovering from the fight. Today he's no longer sleepy or withdrawn, he's up and around and he wants nothing to do with me. He won't tell me to leave, but he doesn't have to. His body said it when I touched him this morning and he flinched. I should be more understanding of what he's going through, but his innate reaction tore through me, shredding my heart in pieces.

I don't want to push him, but I can't help myself. I'm selfish, hating the feeling in my gut, I need to know he's okay. That *we'll* be okay. I have no idea if it will work, but I can't stay here anymore just waiting for him to push me further away. He doesn't acknowledge it when I pack up my bag, I wish his desire for me to stay was stronger. That it would be enough to make him snap out of it as he watches me walk out the door. But instead, he just nods when I tell him I'm going home. I kiss him goodbye on the lips softly, even though he doesn't respond. I want to feel that beautiful mouth on mine one last time before I go, knowing it could be the last after what I'm about to do.

Even though I took a few days off, I go straight to the office from Nico's to talk to Regina, hoping she will support my decision. Lawrence is at the desk when I walk in, and he's smiling. He probably thinks we've been out celebrating. His face falls as I get closer. I'm a mess and I can't even begin to try to hide it.

"Can you take an early lunch?" Regina is standing to go with me before I finish the question. Lawrence doesn't balk when I tell him I need the rest of the week off. I've hardly taken any time since I started and I work twice the amount of hours as most.

Lawrence stops me as I turn to leave with Regina. "Take care of yourself. And keep this one for the rest of the day. I'll get the old ball and chain to come over and work reception. She's been bugging me to spend more time with her anyway…maybe this will count toward my new quota." He tries to make light of his concern for me, but it's written on his face clear as day. Surprising him, I reach up and kiss his cheek before Regina and I take off from the office.

It's true, you really can find anything with Google, and a little determination these days. As soon as I find what I need, I call and set a time to see him the next day. I wish it was today, but it will have to do. Regina stays with me the rest of the night, pretending to fall asleep on my couch, but I know she never planned to leave from the minute she caught sight of me today.

Nico

It's been days since I saw her. At least I think it has. One day just rolls into the next when you lie around and wallow in your own self-pity. She hasn't called since she left and I don't blame her.

Fucking Preach had me believing that the fight would heal me, like getting back in the cage would make me feel whole again, normal. Things were starting to go good for the first time in a long time before I went back. It was my decision, but I'll never forgive Preach for telling me it was right.

I should have just finished what I started, let him pummel me until I was out. But then I started to lift myself from the mat, ready to receive my final penance, when I caught sight of her. It was only a second, but that was all it took. Standing on her chair, screaming and cheering, wearing my face on her t-shirt. I thought it was a sign. A sign that Preach was right and I needed to take back what was mine, to move forward with my life. So I did it. I stood over the brother of the man I killed…the man who looks just like him, and struck another blow. And he didn't move. His head rattled around in slow motion and I watched as he bounced lifelessly from the mat. I thought I'd killed. Again.

Fucking Preach. *Push through, take back your life and move on,* is what he said. Look where it got me. I've showed the first person that I thought understood me in a long time my true colors. I'm a monster. I don't blame her for leaving me.

The bell sounds again from downstairs. I know it's Preach, he's the only one that refuses to god damn listen and leave me alone. So help me God, I may not be able to hold back from beating the shit out of the old guy this time. He's tried my patience and it won't take much to shell out the punishment he deserves. The bastard should be miserable too.

I send the elevator down and wait patiently as it comes back up. I'm done with him and he's gonna know it. Practically ripping the lift gate off the hinges, I throw it open, ready to pounce on Preach. "What the fuck!"

The confused visitor takes a step back, throwing his hands up in surrender. For a second, I'm confused, almost not recognizing the man retreating in my elevator car fully dressed.

"Wooo, man. If it's not a good time, I'll split."

I just stand there, not knowing what to say or do. I'm a little shell-shocked to see him. His face relaxes a little as my anger is replaced by confusion.

"You gonna invite me in, or kick my ass again?" Trevor smiles. His face is bruised and cut, but he's standing there, inside my elevator, looking better than I do.

I finally step aside, motioning silently for him to enter. Trevor walks in and whistles approvingly. "Nice space." I watch as he looks around, his eyes falling to the championship belt that I haven't touched since

Preach threw it at me two days ago. It's sitting on the floor in the living room.

Trevor laughs, "If that was my belt, I'd still be wearing it. Bet that thing can land allota good tits and ass."

I'm not laughing with him when he turns his attention on me, understanding spreading across his face as he speaks. "That's right, you don't need any of that shit. That little lawyer of yours is hot as hell, but sure is a handful. She could sell ice to an eskimo." He shakes his head as if he's reflecting.

My fists clench at my sides at the mention of Elle. Who does this clown think he is walking into my house and talking shit about my girl? Like a good fighter, he reads my face and knows there's trouble coming. Throwing his hands up again in mock surrender, he chirps out, "Take it easy man, I didn't mean nothin' by it. She's a great lady."

"What do you know about Elle?" Throwing your hands up isn't going to make me stop when you talk about Elle, but it will make it easier for me to rip your eyes from the socket so you never check her out again.

"She came to see me, man. I was a perfect gentleman, calm down. I'm not stupid enough to risk a beat down twice from you."

I force myself to relax my balled fists. "Look, I'm lost on what you're talking about. You wanna help me out here?"

Trevor nods. "Your lady came to see me. Filled me in that you're beating yourself up over our fight." He stops and takes a deep breath. "And your fight with my brother."

He's got my attention now. Trevor looks into my eyes, man to man when he continues. "My brother wasn't your fault. We don't blame you. It could have been any fighter in there. Could have happened to any one of us, even me. His head wasn't right. Doctors said it was a slow bleed and could have gone off at any time."

I'm listening to the words, but can't believe they're being spoken. "If I don't blame you, why are you still blaming yourself?" I've no answer for his question either.

"Listen, man. Deep down, I knew I didn't have a shot with you either. But the fight was good for me, gave me the exposure I needed to make a name for myself. You know the grudge crap was all to sell tickets." He walks towards the open elevator, putting his hand on my shoulder as he passes.

Trevor lifts the gate and it looks like he's going to walk out, but then he turns back to me. "Frankie wouldn't want you carrying this around with you. He thought you were the shit. Used to watch you on T.V. all the time, and try to memorize your moves. He'd want you to get your lazy ass back in the cage and show 'em how it's done." He lifts a hand, offering me a wave, and takes a step into the waiting elevator car. "And if that doesn't get your head out of your ass, I'm giving you twenty-four hours to go after the lawyer. If she isn't smiling pretty by then, I'm calling fair game for me trying my hand at putting it back on her face." He slams the gate down, securing the latch. Smart man, putting steel between us after the last comment.

CHAPTER 49

Elle

I've worn a bare patch in the area rug in my living room today. Sometimes the best intentions wind up being the nails that build the house of failure. Trevor said he would go see him, and he sounded genuine, but I'm not even sure if he really did. Worse, what if he did go to him and Nico sees my going behind his back as traitorous... unforgivable.

And then my phone rings and my heart races with hope. But it's quickly stomped on when I see Regina's face flashing on the screen. Not that I don't appreciate her constant checking on me since she left this morning, but it's not the face I long to see on my screen.

Regina wants me to meet her, go to a meeting. I really don't want to, I'm in no mood for cheering up. I prefer to stay home and sulk with my good friends Ben and Jerry. But she's worried about me and that, in turn, means she won't take no for an answer. She's relentless until I finally agree, and in all honesty, I do it just to shut her up. I don't think I need a meeting, but I agree to go anyway because I know she won't sleep tonight if I don't.

Grief counseling meetings are sort of like AA meetings. People come and go, some losing their battle to move past their grief, others succeeding in their efforts and sharing their stories. Regina and I attended meetings in the basement of this community center for more than ten years. For years I attended three times a week, never sharing my story with anyone, but listening to people helped me...knowing I wasn't alone in my battle. It's where I met Regina.

Her husband was killed in a horrific accident, where the driver was under the influence and the passenger was severely injured. Unfortunately, her husband was the driver and she was the passenger. So many people tried to help me over the years, but it was Regina who I finally connected with. We were both racked with guilt and shame, spending all our energy trying to forget what happened in our lives. She helped me take baby steps forward when I thought I needed to run backwards.

I recognize a few faces as we take our seats in the back row, some have been here for ten years like us, for others it may be their first time. Anyone can share their story, there's supposed to be no judgment between members. After ten minutes, I start to relax. As much as I hate to admit it, Regina was right for bringing me here. The past few days have opened up old wounds, and there is comfort in hearing the leader's kind words on forgiveness. It also makes me think I did the right thing with Nico, even if he doesn't recognize it. I'd rather him heal and hate me than suffer and stand by my side.

The usual group leader announces a new member would like to speak. We're reminded of the phone's off rule, and I'm still digging in my disorganized bag in search of my phone when the voice hits me. I know it's him, but when I look up I still can't believe what my eyes are seeing. He doesn't look up as he speaks quietly.

"A smart woman told me to come here months ago...but I was too stubborn to listen."

Nico inhales deeply, pushing a loud breath out before he begins, his face still looking down.

"Eighteen months ago I killed a man. I didn't intend to, but it happened anyway. I'm a fighter and it happened in the cage. The ref ruled it a clean hit, but it doesn't change that it was my hand that dealt him the blow that killed him.

I've spent the last year of my life under a cloud of guilt and shame. I went on, going through the motions every day, but I was dead too. I grieved for the loss of the man, and the loss of who I was. For a whole year. A year of my life that I can't get back. But it wasn't until today that I realized I even lost it."

Nico pauses and I hold my breath as I watch his head slowly rise. His eyes find mine instantly, just like every other time. Everything else in the room disappears and it's as if we're the only two in a long tunnel, sitting on opposites ends, but inexplicably drawn to each other.

"Then today I was given a gift. A gift by an amazing woman. She gave me the gift of forgiveness because I thought that was what I needed to move on. But I was wrong. No one was keeping me from moving on, only me. She taught me more about fighting for what you want than I'd learned spending half my life in the cage. I finally get it…what makes us move on is to accept what we feel and share it."

Nico's voice becomes shaky and I fight the urge to go comfort him, but I can't hold back the stream of tears that fall from my face silently.

"Today I made peace with it, Babe. And you gave that to me. I only wish there was something I could give you back that meant as much as what you did for me. But there isn't one thing big enough to call it even. So if you'll have me, I want to spend the next fifty or sixty years trying to repay you…saying thank you every day. Because you, lady, are all I need."

My feet can't get to him fast enough. I almost knock over two rows of folding chairs in front of me, trying to make my way. But when I finally do, he holds me so tight that everything else fades away and I know we're going to be okay. As long as we have each other.

EPILOGUE

Six months later

Elle

It's almost one on Saturday afternoon when I leave the office. Nico asked me to come to the gym to help him with something. He's being elusive, won't tell me what it's all about. There's a bit of a knot in my stomach as I drive, hoping I'm not going to be hearing bad news. The last six months have been the happiest time in my life. I hadn't even realized what I'd been missing till I met Nico Hunter. But he has another fight coming up soon and I worry he may have heard news that could push him back. We've made such progress, individually and as a couple. Both of us finally putting our past in its place and moving forward...together. We don't try to drown it out anymore, like it or not, our past is our own, and it's made us who we are today. Accept and move on.

I'm surprised when I find the gym almost empty. Usually on Saturdays the place is filled with guys with no necks. Sal's at the front desk and tells me Nico's waiting for me in the storage room. The storage room is a big open space, almost half the size of the gym, only it's unfinished and bare, with a few metal shelves lining the walls and some decade-old file cabinets. Nico must be filing paperwork, something he dreads and lets pile up for way too long.

The storage room is dark when I open the door and I'm just about to pull the door shut when a nameplate on the door catches my eye. *The Women's Annex.* I don't recall ever seeing it before and certainly I would have remembered anything that has to do with women in this macho male gym.

Curiosity gets the best of me, so I reach in and switch on the light, stunned at the vision I find before my eyes as they adjust from the darkness. What once looked like an oversized garage is now completely refinished. The walls are painted a pale pink, there's rubber matting on the floor, similar to the black ones in the gym, but these are light grey, less obtrusive. Pictures hang on the walls, most of women in gym clothes exercising and kickboxing. To my right, there's a wall lined with exercise equipment, all sparkling chrome, shiny and new. Large mirrors cover the walls behind the equipment and movement in its reflection catches my eye and startles me for a second. I turn to my left following the reflection and find Nico standing in the doorway of a room, a room that wasn't even there the last time I was in here to grab some supplies.

"Confused?" Nico grins at me, he looks pleased to find that I am.

"When did you do all this? And why didn't you mention you were getting work done?"

"Because I wanted it to be a surprise."

"It's beautiful." I look around, taking in the entirety of the transformation. It really is pretty. Different from the muscle head gym that stands on the other side of the door. It looks soft and inviting, not hard and intimidating. "But it looks so…different from the rest of the gym?"

Nico chuckles. "That's because it is different, Babe."

"It's a women's gym?"

"Sort of." Pushing his body from the door frame, Nico walks to me. I stand and watch as he comes towards me, knowing he won't leave any distance between us, he'll invade my space. And he does. He stops directly in front of me, close enough so that the hairs on my arms raise and my body responds to his nearness. I'll never tire of what this man does to me.

Nico wraps his hand around my neck, pulling me in for a quick kiss on the lips, releasing me only enough so I can see his face, but our bodies are still touching when he continues. "This is the new women's self defense center. I worked it out with Janna over at the battered women's shelter you volunteer at. I'm going to teach classes three nights a week, after the fight gym closes, get women to learn how to defend themselves."

I don't know what to say for a minute, it's rare I'm actually rendered speechless. Nico doesn't move. Instead he waits, giving me time to collect my thoughts. His thumb rubs soothingly up and down the back of my neck while I let it all sink in. "You did this for me?" The words come out as a whisper, a thought that escaped my mouth.

"I did it for us. I couldn't be there for you and your mom when you needed help. I know it makes no sense, but I'll never forgive myself for not being there for you then. But I can try to be there for the next woman who needs to defend herself." Nico pauses, searching my eyes for something intently. "You changed my life, gave me peace. I promised you I'd spend the rest of my life trying to give back to you what you gave me. This is just the start."

"I...I don't know what to say."

"Say you like it, Babe."

"I like it, Babe." I smile up at the towering tough guy looking down at me so sweetly.

"That's good. Because you're going to be my assistant." He grins like a Cheshire cat.

I raise my eyebrows in surprise. "I am?"

"Yep, I'm going to put my hands all over that body of yours in the front of the room and you're going to kick my ass."

I reach up, locking my hands behind his neck. Doing my best impression of serious, "I'm not sure I can do that."

Nico looks concerned and for a second I feel badly for screwing with him.

"I'm sorry, Babe, if it's too hard…"

"Oh, if it's hard, I'm definitely not sure I can do it…" I grin.

A look of relief passes over his face, but it's replaced quickly by something else…and that something else looks devilish. "Oh, it's always hard for you, Babe." He yanks me tighter against him, demonstrating his words are spoken with truth as I feel his thick erection push into me. "Let's go christen our new office."

"Our new office?"

"Yep, I was going to give you the full tour, but now that's going to have to wait till later. Much later."

And we do. We christen the new office…and the new supply room, and the floor…

Three more months later…

Elle

So much has changed in the past year. Nico is still the champion, but now we celebrate after a fight. We've started a new tradition of having a party the night after a win at Nico's gym. Neither one of us looks back to the time where winning a fight only caused pain.

My mom even came to the party tonight. She wasn't ready to see the fight, but we're working our way up to it. Baby steps, no more running backwards. I watch as Nico's crazy nephews spar in the ring wearing head gear three sizes too big for them. Preach, of course, in one corner with one eight year old, and Nico coaching in the other. And the ref? Well that's Vinny, of course.

Tonight we're going to tell our families that we're getting married. I wish I had a romantic story to share, maybe that he proposed on a hot air balloon ride, or slipped a fortune requesting my hand in marriage into a fortune cookie. But I've agreed to marry Nico, the black and blue, hotter than hell heavyweight champion, not some pansy Price Charming. So instead, for the rest of my life I'll blush when I think of how the man I'm crazy in love with proposed to me.

Nico

There's not a dry damn eye in the house when I announce that Elle agreed to marry me last night. She made me swear not to share that I fucked her into agreeing to marry me. But damn if she didn't scream yes at least a half dozen times as her orgasm took us both over the edge last night.

It might not have been traditional, but it's the way I want to remember the happiest moment of my life, so to hell with tradition… we'll make our own. I had flowers and a bent down on one knee proposal all planned out for today before the party, but like a good fighter, I saw the moment, changed things up on the fly, and went for it. I couldn't help myself. I walked into my bedroom and she was laying in bed and smiled up at me. With the sun setting, the red sky filtered in through the open window and cast a shadow around her. And there she was again. My angel. So I made love to her and told her how I felt. That I'd never been happier in my life, that she was my angel and I wanted to wake up to her every day for the rest of my life. Give her my name and make it official, although in my heart it was already a done deal.

The women surround her and ooh and aah at her ring and start asking her a million questions about the wedding, even though it just happened last night. She catches me staring and smiles at me. It's her big goofy smile, the one that I know she can't fake… and it's all for me. Two years ago, I didn't think I'd ever have peace in my life again. But today as I look around the room, I realize I have so much more. I may not ever accept I deserve what I have, but it's mine all the same.

I smile back at Elle as Preach approaches me, slapping his arm on my shoulder as he stands next to me taking everything I'm seeing in.

"You're one lucky bastard." The old man has a way with words.

"I sure am. And I'll never forget it again."

Eight more months later...

Elle

I'm still floating after the last few days. Our wedding was everything I could have dreamed of, and then some. I'll never forget the look on Nico's face when our eyes locked as I stood at the back of the aisle. There had to be at least two hundred people who turned to watch me take the slow walk down to the altar, but I didn't see a single one of them. Everything else became a blur, except the smile on Nico's face. The face that watched my every step was crystal clear to me, showing every emotion he was feeling. Emotions that mirrored mine. Emotions that I finally welcomed.

The sound of the waves hitting the beach as we walk fills my ears. Warm water wets my feet with every wave and I can't wait for it to wash over me again when it recedes. Kauai is beautiful, a perfect place for a honeymoon. But it doesn't hold a candle to the handsome face that smiles at me as we walk hand in hand down the beach in the late afternoon sun.

Then I catch a glimpse of my shadow, and what I see takes my breath away. I'm no longer running from something that doesn't exist. I don't have to. I don't see my own ghost in a shadow when I look down, I see Nico. His shadow looms over us both. It's big and it's bold and it towers over mine protectively. Just like the man.

Dear Readers,

If you liked Nico and Elle, then please check out Vince & Liv in 2014. Nico's protégé, Vinny, is all grown up, but the chaos of his childhood still swirls around him. The MMA Fighter series continues in *Worth the Chance*, the story of

Vince "The Invinnnciiibbble" Stone.

Add Worth the Chance to your reading list here:

http://www.goodreads.com/book/show/18080889-worth-the-fight

OTHER BOOKS BY VI KEELAND

Life on Stage series (2 standalone books)
Beat
Throb

MMA Fighter series (3 standalone books)
Worth the Chance
Worth Forgiving

The Cole Series (2 book serial)
Belong to You
Made for You

Standalone novels
Cocky Bastard (Co-written with Penelope Ward)
Left Behind (A Young Adult Novel)
First Thing I See

AUTHOR LINKS

Facebook: https://www.facebook.com/pages/Author-Vi-Keeland/435952616513958

Website: http://www.vikeeland.com

Twitter: https://twitter.com/ViKeeland

Instagram: http://instagram.com/Vi_Keeland/

Pinterest: http://www.pinterest.com/vikeeland/pins/

Goodreads: http://www.goodreads.com/author/show/6887119.Vi_Keeland

Amazon Author Page: http://www.amazon.com/Vi-Keeland/e/B00AZJ8TT0/

Mailing List Signup: http://eepurl.com/brAPo9

ACKNOWLEDGEMENTS

Thank you to all of the bloggers that generously give their time to read and support Indie Authors! I am well aware that, without all of your help spreading the word on my books, the popularity of my stories would not be the same.

A special thank you to three special women that have done so much to help me get my stories out. Nita (The BookChick Blog Reviews), Andrea, & Jen (RomCon)– Thank you for beta reading, editing, making kick-ass trailers, beautiful covers, being my sounding boards and mostly for your honesty!

Finally, thank you so much to all the readers. It is so much fun to create stories when you have amazing readers to love your characters. Keep your notes coming, I truly love hearing from you!

All my best,
Vi

CPSIA information can be obtained
at www.ICGtesting.com
Printed in the USA
LVOW03s1437301117
558160LV00012B/1175/P

9 781682 304228